"Do I frighten you, Harriet?" He bent his mouth to hers, ignoring her faint murmur of protest.

His lips were firm and cool and Harriet stayed unresisting in the circle of his arms, accepting the embrace stoically, waiting for it to end.

But his lips grew warmer and more insistent and began to move against her own, and all at once, she felt that dizzying sweetness starting somewhere in the pit of her stomach and spreading through her whole body. He pressed her tightly against him until she could not tell where his body began and hers ended....

TO DREAM OF LOVE

Marion Chesney

FAWCETT CREST • NEW YORK

A Fawcett Crest Book
Published by Ballantine Books
Copyright © 1986 by Marion Chesney

Library of Congress Catalog Card Number: 86-90871

ISBN 0-449-20532-0

Manufactured in the United States of America

First Edition: June 1986

For Tom and Eileen Kerr
With love

Chapter One

It was a very cold spring, one that Harriet Clifton was to remember for the rest of her life. For that spring was to be the turning point in her young life.

Harriet lived a life of genteel poverty in a large, rambling house on the outskirts of the village of Lower Maxton in the county of Brent. The house was all that was left of the once great Clifton fortune. Her father, Mr. James Clifton, had been an inveterate gambler, and when he had died of typhoid, he had left his wife only a small annuity to go with the great mansion. Mrs. Clifton, always weak and ailing, had followed her husband to the grave two short months later. Harriet and her elder sister, Cordelia, were left in the charge of an elderly spinster aunt, Miss Rebecca Clifton, their late father's sister.

At the time of their mother's death, Cordelia was eighteen and Harriet eleven. Cordelia was a strong-willed beauty, impatient with the new regime of pov-

1

erty. Cordelia had caught the attention of a rich neighbor, Charles, Lord Bentley. When she announced her engagement to him, Harriet and her aunt had felt sure that life would take a more comfortable turn.

But Cordelia seemed to forget about them as soon as the ring was on her finger. Her lord died after only six months of marriage, leaving Cordelia everything. She shocked the county by selling the Bentley house and estates, lock, stock, and barrel. She then moved to London and continued to ignore the existence of her younger sister and elderly aunt.

Harriet was now eighteen and, up until that cold spring of 1811, had philosophically accepted that Cordelia would continue to ignore them.

The Clifton mansion was called Pringle House, retaining the name of a previous owner who had died the century before.

Harriet's aunt did not know how to make ends meet. One by one, the stately rooms were locked up after their contents had been sold.

One after the other, the servants had been dismissed until there was only Harriet and her aunt living in a small portion of the house while dampness invaded the unheated rooms, and the gardens and grounds outside turned into a wilderness of thorns and weeds.

Harriet had dug up a strip of the south lawn and planted vegetables and had turned another strip into a hen run. She tried to cheer Aunt Rebecca by pointing out that at least they had fresh eggs and vegetables, but it was hard to be grateful for anything when there was nothing they could do to alleviate the damp cold that seemed to creep into their very bones.

Her hands were blistered and cracked with sawing and chopping of logs from fallen trees.

Harriet longed passionately for summer as a cold wind continued to blow from the east, bringing flurries of snow to whiten the tangled mass of what had once been one of the most beautiful gardens in England.

Pringle House had been badly built. The walls were cracked, and the floors sagged. The kitchen fire smoked abominably, and the drawing-room fire, before it had become blocked with soot, had sent all heat roaring straight up to the roof.

March the twenty-fifth was a particularly vile day.

Harriet knew the kitchen fire was almost completely blocked with soot. It was possible to live without the drawing-room fire, but the kitchen was another matter, since this past winter it had served as drawing room and dining room as well as kitchen. Harriet could not afford to pay a sweep, so that morning she scaled the roof and poked various brooms tied together with string down the old chimney. The resultant fall of soot blackened everything in the kitchen. Aunt Rebecca went into strong hysterics and retired to her chilly bedchamber, leaving Harriet to clear up the mess.

Harriet worked grimly on throughout the morning until the kitchen was sparkling again.

Looking at herself in the cracked glass on the kitchen wall, she saw to her dismay that she was as black as any sweep.

The kitchen fire was blazing cheerfully for the first time in years, but the thought of boiling kettle after kettle of water to fill a bath seemed just too much of an effort to the exhausted Harriet. Besides, Aunt Rebecca would be horrified at the very idea of *anyone* taking a full bath for anything other than medicinal purposes.

Harriet stared moodily at her soot-streaked face in the glass. Clear gray, heavy-lashed eyes stared back.

Her black hair, dull black now with soot, hung in heavy, tangled masses almost to her waist. She felt gritty and filthy all over.

She trailed out to the pump in the yard and began to pump water energetically into a leather bucket.

Then an idea came to her. There was no one for miles around, and Aunt Rebecca would not quit her room until she was sure the kitchen was clean. Why not strip everything off and scrub down under the pump? It would only take a few freezing minutes, and then she could run indoors and rub herself dry in front of the kitchen fire.

She went back into the house and into the small maid's room at the back of the kitchen where she slept—the large bedrooms on the upper floors being too vast to heat. She laid out clean underwear, yellowed and darned, a well-worn woolen round gown, coarse gray stockings, and a clean calico pinafore, then carried the lot into the kitchen and piled them on a chair in front of the fire to warm.

Then she removed all of her dirty, sooty clothes and placed them in a basket in the corner, ready for washing.

She took a deep breath. If she stayed much longer in front of the fire, she might lose her courage. Stark naked, clutching a bar of cheap laundry soap, she ran out of the kitchen and into the yard, seized the pump handle, and let out a yell as the first flood of icy water struck her bare skin.

She soaped and scrubbed furiously until she was sure there was not a single particle of soot left in her hair or on her body.

It was when she was turning away from the pump to make her dash back to the kitchen that she realized there was a man on horseback watching her.

Frozen to the spot, not with cold but with shock, she stared up at him.

He had a hard, high-nosed aristocratic face and a quantity of fashionably cut hair as black as hers. His hazel eyes raked over her body from head to foot, and an appreciative smile curved his lips. He held his hat in one hand, and as she stared at him, eyes wide with shock, he raised it in a salute.

Harriet gave a little scream and then ran for the kitchen door, hurtling inside and then barring and bolting it behind her.

She could *feel* herself turning scarlet with shame and embarrassment, blushing from the soles of her feet to the top of her head. She rubbed herself dry as quickly as possible and scrambled into her clean clothes, then twisted the damp masses of her black hair up into a knot.

She crept to the kitchen window and looked out. There was no sign of the stranger. She had not heard him ride off, but the thick, shaggy grass was wet and spongy and had probably muffled the sounds of his departure.

There were shuffling, coughing sounds that heralded the approach of Aunt Rebecca. Harriet decided to tell her nothing about the visit of the strange man. Aunt would dissolve into hysterics again, and Harriet felt she could not bear more than one attack of them a day. Besides, the gentleman had probably lost his way and would no doubt think her some servant girl.

The kitchen door opened and Aunt Rebecca walked in. She was a large, amorphous lump of a woman whose weak, washed-out blue eyes gazed myopically out of a great, moonlike face. Her lank brown hair fell in wisps about her face from under a grayish white cap.

Harriet was never quite sure which gown her aunt was wearing, because that lady was so set about with brooches and trinkets, shawls and scarves, it was hard to make out what was underneath. She smelled strongly of camphor and woodsmoke. She had an incipient mustache. She was silly, fussy, and complained constantly about the delicate state of her nerves.

And Harriet loved her dearly.

Underneath all her spasms and hysterics, Aunt Rebecca was warm and loving. She always declared that Harriet was much prettier than Cordelia, and although Harriet knew that no one could compete with Cordelia's glorious, golden beauty, she found her aunt's championship very comforting.

"How pretty you have made things!" exclaimed Aunt Rebecca, blinking shortsightedly at the well-scrubbed kitchen. "And such a fire! It warms my heart. You are such a *resolute* girl, Harriet."

Harriet gave her a shaky smile. She was still feeling upset and ashamed.

Revived by the warmth, Aunt Rebecca picked up the heavy iron kettle, hung it on the idle-back, and swung it over the small, bright fire. The kitchen fire was in the center of a black range. It had an oven on one side, a boiler on the other, and a roasting spit set in front.

"Do you think," she asked, "that we might just have a little *real* tea?"

"I do not see why we should deprive ourselves," said Harriet. "We have been saving it for visitors, but no one ever calls now." Then she remembered the stranger and turned her face away to hide a guilty blush.

Aunt Rebecca brought down a japanned canister from a shelf and peered inside. "Just enough," she murmured.

Harriet and her aunt normally drank tea made from fennel leaves. China tea was kept for visitors. But no one had called for quite some time, and even the vicar seemed to have forgotten about them.

Aunt Rebecca pulled a chair close to the fire and sat down, waiting for the kettle to boil. Harriet lifted the lid of the flour bin and debated whether to make some cakes to celebrate the unusual luxury of having "real" tea.

The knocker on the front door began to sound loudly. Both stiffened in surprise and looked at each other.

"Dear me," said Aunt Rebecca. "Now, who can that be?"

Harriet thought of the stranger. She carefully replaced the lid of the flour bin. "If we do not answer, Aunt, then whoever it is might go away."

"Go *away!*" exclaimed Aunt Rebecca, heaving her bulk out of the chair. "My precious child, we have not seen anyone these past two months. I will go."

"Let it be the vicar," prayed Harriet aloud as her aunt waddled out of the kitchen. But Harriet had not really much hope that it would prove to be the vicar. The church of St. Edmund lay in the center of Lower Maxton, which was a good ten miles away. Harriet and her aunt had ceased to attend. Their last visit had been the previous year. They had been badly snubbed by the local county as usual, not because of the shabbiness of their clothes but because of their relationship to the wicked Cordelia, Lady Bentley, who had sold the Bentley estate to a Welsh ironmaster. Even old Lady Humphries had said loudly that she was surprised they did not look more prosperous, since they were noted for their success in encouraging the growth of *mushrooms* in the county, a cutting reference to the parvenu ironmaster.

The ironmaster himself eagerly emulated the cruelty of the class to which he hoped to aspire and told his wife sharply to "come away" when it looked as if she might speak to Aunt Rebecca. Harriet had felt she could not bear to see any of them again, and Aunt Rebecca had sadly agreed.

The vicar had dutifully called at Pringle House, but the man of society was obviously having such a struggle with the man of the cloth, and a painful one at that, that Harriet had told him tartly not to put himself out of his way by paying them any visits in the future.

Harriet could now hear the sound of voices in the hall. She did not want to leave the security of the kitchen, in case she might find herself in the company of the hard-eyed stranger.

But whoever had called had obviously been invited in. The drawing-room fire would need to be made up, and, alas, their precious little reserve of tea offered to this most unwelcome guest or guests.

Harriet took off her apron and smoothed down her old gown with nervous fingers.

Unlike the more modern houses in the county, the kitchen of Pringle House was not in the basement. She walked along a stone-flagged passage and entered the hall, trying not to notice the familiar bareness of it and the still-clean squares on the walls that showed where the pictures had been taken down and sold.

She pushed open the door of the drawing room. A brooding, morose, Byronic-looking young man was lounging in an armchair. Apart from a colored Belcher neckerchief, he was dressed entirely in black. His hair was worn long and was of an indeterminate shade of brown, and his large brown eyes were sullen. Harriet judged him to be only a little older than she. Aunt

Harriet had perched her bulk on a small chair facing him.

Crouched in front of the fire and in the process of lighting it was a tall man. Harriet could only see the back of his head and his broad shoulders under a well-tailored blue coat.

"My niece, Miss Harriet Clifton," said Aunt Rebecca with simple pride. The morose young man jumped to his feet and executed a low bow.

The man who was lighting the fire stood up and turned about. Mocking hazel eyes fastened on Harriet. She blushed painfully. The stranger from the kitchen garden!

"Your servant, Miss Clifton," he said. He raised an inquiring eyebrow at Aunt Rebecca, who was nodding and smiling in agreement, although no one had said anything to agree with.

A flash of humor lit the hazel eyes. "I see I must make the introductions," he said. "The tortured gentleman over there with a dark soul is my cousin, Mr. Bertram Hudson. I am Arden."

"The Marquess of Arden," prompted Aunt Rebecca, who knew her peerage inside out.

"The same, ma'am. Now, if you will excuse me, I will soon have a comfortable blaze."

Mr. Hudson slumped back down into his chair, Aunt Rebecca continued to nod and smile like a large clock-work doll, and Harriet stood where she was, nervously pleating a fold in her dress with her work-reddened fingers.

The fire blazed up and then settled down into a depressingly smoky mass.

"The fire does not draw very well," said Harriet, her voice sounding strangely muffled and odd in her own ears.

"You obviously do not use this room very much," said the marquess, fastidiously dusting his long white fingers on a cambric handkerchief.

He gazed thoughtfully about the room, from the thread-bare brocade curtains to the damp-stained walls, and then at the bare boards of the floor.

"No, my lord," said Harriet. "I fear we are sadly short of comfortable rooms in which to entertain anyone." Her eyes pleaded with him not to mention seeing her under the pump. He studied her thought-fully and then nodded slightly in answer to her un-spoken request.

"Then where *do* you warm yourselves?" drawled Mr. Hudson.

"It is of no consequence," said Harriet, disliking the lounging young man. "I fear we are unable to offer you hospitality, gentleman. So if you will inform me of the reason for your call, I will do my best to be of assistance."

"But the *tea*," said Aunt Rebecca in a stage whis-per. "We have *tea*."

"We lost our way to the London road," said the marquess. "I tried to pull the bell earlier, and when I did not get any reply, I rode around to the back of the house to see if I could see anyone." He looked steadily at Harriet. "But there was no one in sight. I would have left without trying again, but something happened. I regret to tell you that my cousin, believing the estate to be abandoned, shot two of your hens."

Harriet bit her lip. She had been about to cry out in fury. She had only six hens, and the killing of two of them was a sore loss. She said aloud, "But I did not hear any shots. Did you, Aunt Rebecca?"

"I was asleep, more like," said Aunt Rebecca.

"Perhaps *you* were so busy you did not hear, Miss Harriet," said the marquess, a smile beginning to curl his lips.

Harriet remembered how the water had gushed out of the pump, effectively drowning out any sound, and blushed painfully.

"And so," went on the marquess, "after I learned of the murder, I returned and tried the door knocker instead, feeling sure the bellpull was broken. Here we are to make amends. We have two hens, dead, I am afraid, and a hamper of delicacies that we beg you to accept to show our true remorse."

Mr. Hudson sat up. "But that hamper was a pre—"

The marquess's steely voice cut across his. "*And* you will be paid handsomely for the loss of your birds."

"There is no need, no need at all to pay anything," said Harriet. "Mr. Hudson made an understandable mistake."

"I was only having a bit of sport," grumbled Mr. Hudson. "Thought the place had been deserted this age."

"I insist," said the marquess. "Bertram, go and tell John and Peter to carry in the hamper."

Bertram Hudson slouched out with a lowering look.

"I think if I had some dry logs, I might yet be able to build a blaze," said the marquess.

"Certainly," said Harriet with a quelling look at Aunt Rebecca. "I will tell our butler to arrange the matter."

Aunt Rebecca emitted faint noises of distress from among her shawls, but Harriet marched firmly from the room.

She had used up the inside stock of logs for the kitchen fire. She threw a shawl over her shoulders, tied on the apron that she had removed before going into the drawing room, and went out of the kitchen door. The pump stood there in the chilly light, a mute reminder of her indecency.

She went around to the old pinking shed, which was filled with dead tree trunks that she had dragged into shelter.

"Why did I not think to chop more logs this morning?" muttered Harriet, seizing the axe.

She was chopping away busily when a calm voice behind her said, "Allow me, Miss Harriet."

Will I *ever* stop blushing? thought Harriet miserably as the Marquess of Arden's broad shoulders filled the doorway.

He shrugged himself out of his coat and hung it up on a nail, then took the axe from Harriet's unresisting fingers.

"I am afraid I had forgotten it was the servants' day off," lied Harriet. "Please do not trouble . . ."

"It is no trouble," he said, expertly wielding the axe.

Harriet watched with something approaching envy as a neat pile of logs and kindling began to appear before her eyes. She wondered how he kept his hands so white, since he obviously knew how to use an axe, and the thin cambric of his shirt revealed the play of strong muscles in his back.

"There!" He stacked a large basket with logs and kindling and nodded to her to lead the way.

He stopped in the kitchen and looked slowly around. The kettle was singing on the hearth, steam whistling through a hole in its old iron lid. Brightly colored plates, very few of them matching, shone from a Welsh dresser. Aunt Rebecca's knitting was lying on the kitchen table at one end and a little pile of Harriet's favorite books was at the other.

"We shall not stay very long, Miss Harriet," said the marquess. "Perhaps we would all be more comfortable in the kitchen. Your servants do themselves very well."

But from the glint in his eye, Harriet was well aware that the marquess had not for a moment believed her lie about the servants' day off.

"I will fetch Aunt," she said with a little sigh. The marquess was so tall and elegant and carefree that Harriet suddenly envied her sister, Cordelia, from the bottom of her heart. Cordelia belonged to the same world as the marquess, a world of scent and warmth, hot food, well-trained servants, and beautiful clothes.

"Oh, and incidentally, Miss Harriet," said the marquess. Harriet turned at the door and looked around. "I am notoriously shortsighted and I have quite an appalling memory."

Harriet looked at him intently, but the hazel eyes were grave and steady. "Thank you," she said quietly.

When she returned, she was followed by her aunt, Mr. Hudson, and the marquess's servants, who were bearing a hamper.

"Put it on the table," said the marquess. "And John, ride to the nearest village and bring back a sweep. Double wages if he comes quickly." He turned to Aunt Rebecca. "Your drawing-room fire will blaze very merrily once the chimney is unblocked, ma'am."

"I do not know how to thank you," said Aunt Rebecca, quite overset. "That a gentleman such as you should see to what straits we . . ."

"Madam," said the marquess firmly. "In that hamper are six bottles of the best port. I am going to open and decant one now. We will all feel much warmer after a glass."

As the marquess decanted the wine, Mr. Hudson, much animated by the warmth and the prospect of a glass of port, began to unpack the rest of the hamper, laying the contents out on the kitchen tables. Harriet gazed in a dazed way at all the luxuries that were appearing out of that seemingly bottomless hamper. There was a Westphalia ham, cakes and biscuits of every description, cold pheasant, and loaves of fresh crusty bread.

"This is rather fun," announced Mr. Hudson, looking younger and more boyish by the minute. "We shall have a party."

"That's the ticket." The marquess grinned. "Serve the ladies, Bertram."

The "murdered" hens were hung on a hook in the scullery, and Harriet and Aunt Rebecca settled down to a most enjoyable meal. The party was interrupted at one point by the return of John with the sweep, and Holland covers had to be found to protect the meager furniture in the drawing room.

The marquess talked lightly and easily of the happenings of the day. The newly appointed regent would not enjoy all the power of his father, George III. But he *could* form a government. He had been expected to favor the Whigs and had startled everyone by coming down on the side of the Tories. This brought him many enemies: the Whigs hating him and the Tories still distrusting him. The regent had become deeply religious— although no one expected it to last—and read a chapter or two of the Bible daily with his favorite mistress, Lady Hereford.

Mellowed by food and wine, Mr. Hudson confessed

to ambitions to emulate Lord Byron and read them several of his own poems. Aunt Rebecca assured him that he was *much* better than Lord Byron, and Harriet, who thought the poems were rather dreadful, nonetheless added her praise, since she was relieved to see that the moody Mr. Hudson had a cheerful side to his character.

At one point, Mr. Hudson showed alarming signs of beginning to ask them why they lived in such poverty, but a warning glance from the marquess silenced him.

Harriet did not mention Cordelia, because, for the first time, she was realizing the full enormity of her sister's selfishness and did not even want to speak her name.

Aunt Rebecca did not mention Cordelia either, for fear of being snubbed by this magnificent marquess in the way she had been snubbed in church.

More port was drunk to celebrate the relighting of the now-swept drawing-room fire. Seeing a spinet in the corner of the room, Mr. Hudson begged Harriet to sing them a song. The spinet had not been sold because half of the keyboard was stuck down with damp.

Emboldened by the wine, Harriet sang several pretty ballads in a pleasant soprano. Her hair was now dry, and the one pin, which had proved adequate to keep it up on the top of her head when her hair was wet, finally gave way.

Her black hair tumbled down about her shoulders, and with an embarrassed laugh, she tried to put it up again, finally spreading her hands in a gesture of resignation.

The two men stood watching her as she twisted around on the seat of the spinet, the glory of her hair hanging to her waist.

" 'Her beauty made the bright world dim, and everything beside seemed like the fleeting image of a shade,' " quoted Mr. Hudson in a half whisper.

"We must take our leave," said the marquess, his eyes suddenly hooded by his heavy lids. "Make your bow, Bertram."

Harriet murmured an excuse and fled from the drawing room. In her bedroom, she twisted her hair up into a tight knot and pinned it securely.

When she returned to the hall, both men were taking their leave of Aunt Rebecca, who was telling them the best way to reach the London road.

"Do you come to London, Miss Harriet?" asked Mr. Hudson intensely.

"I am afraid not," said Harriet.

"Then I shall . . ."

"Bertram!" The marquess's voice held a warning. "We are keeping the ladies standing in the cold."

Mr. Hudson threw his cousin a furious look before turning to make his bow to Harriet and Aunt Rebecca.

The marquess bowed. "Good-bye, Miss Harriet," he said. "Perhaps we shall meet again."

"I doubt it," said Harriet wearily, remembering all the social snubs of the county. This aristocrat had obviously found his visit amusing, but he would not wish to return simply to see two such unfashionable and poverty-stricken ladies.

He looked at her with something like pity, opened his mouth as if to say more, closed it again, put on his curly-brimmed beaver, and followed his young cousin out into the twilight.

Harriet closed the door behind them.

"There is a full moon tonight," said Aunt Rebecca, "so we need not feel guilty about their staying so late.

For a moment, dear Harriet, it was like the old days. Your dear mama loved company, and my poor brother, your papa, always had the house full of young men. It is going to be very hard to return to our old ways after such a holiday. Men are so *useful*."

"Money is so useful." Harriet sighed. "Come back to the kitchen, Aunt. It is too cold in the drawing room. All the heat still goes right up the chimney, even though it has just been swept. We have all those delicious treats from the hamper to keep us merry for quite some time."

Aunt Rebecca brightened. "There are even *two* canisters of tea, one India and one China. I fear the hamper had been given to them by whoever it was they had been staying with. I thought Mr. Hudson was quite taken with you, Harriet."

"Yes," agreed Harriet, leading the way to the kitchen. "He had had more than enough to drink. Lord Arden took him away smartish to avoid any embarrassment."

In the kitchen, they set to work to store away all the groceries and meat. The bottom of the hamper was lined with newspapers.

"They are quite recent," said Harriet. "Only a month old. A newspaper is a rare luxury. There is half a decanter of port in the drawing room. I will fetch it, and we can toast our toes in front of the fire and find out how the great world is getting along."

Harriet returned not only with the port but with the blazing remains of the drawing room-fire on a shovel, which she added to the kitchen fire.

"Do read to me," said Aunt Rebecca. "My poor eyes are too weak."

Harriet smiled and smoothed out one of the newspapers. "What do you wish to hear about, Aunt Rebecca? The war in the Peninsula? The new regent?"

"No, the social gossip. I want to hear all about the balls and parties and what everyone was wearing."

"Very well. Good heavens! Here is intelligence of Cordelia. It says: 'Lady Bentley still shines, although our great metropolis is thin of company. At the opera, she caused more eyes to turn in her direction than Catalini. That famous singer was quite eclipsed by our modish beauty, whose shining hair, dressed à la Titus, outshone the glory of the Bentley diamonds.' "

Harriet slowly lowered the paper. "Do you realize, Aunt," she said in a thin, little voice, "that just one, just one tiny little Bentley diamond could keep us in modest comfort for quite a long time?"

"Dear, dear, haven't I often thought so? But you know, Harriet, it does not do to be thinking of such things. That leads to self-pity, and self-pity is such an uncomfortable state of mind, rather like the colic. My delicate nervous system will not stand self-pity or bad thoughts. Is there any gossip?"

"Plenty. Oh, if I am not mistaken, here is Cordelia again, although it refers to her as Lady B. Can the M. of A. be the Marquess of Arden?"

Aunt Rebecca flicked through the pages of the peerage in her mind. "Bound to be," she said at last. "Depends, of course, what the gossip is about. There is the Marquess of Anstruther, but he is in his dotage—not that that would deter Cordelia."

"It is all rather nasty," said Harriet. "No one will ever forgive Cordelia for selling the Bentley estates, and at such a profit. They would rather she had lost them at the gaming tables and then shot herself like a respectable member of the ton. It says here: 'Can the famous estates of the M. of A. be at risk? As well as his notoriously flinty heart? Rumor hath it that our noble peer is enamored of the fair Lady B., who is well known for her agility in disposing of landed estates. Let us hope that the M. of A. loses only his bachelordom, and not his *shirt* as well.' ''

''Oh, how cruel!''

''I cannot see Cordelia caring what anyone says of her . . . provided she gets what she wants. Do you think our marquess would be enamored of such as Cordelia?''

''Of course,'' said Aunt Rebecca simply. ''There was never a man who was not.''

Harriet scowled horribly. This one little party, this short intrusion of the fashionable world into her own life, had brought color and magic—and discontent. The long, empty days of cold and hunger stretched ahead. Cordelia had never known what it was to be hungry or cold. She had ruthlessly sold all the best items in Pringle House to supply herself with a wardrobe to dazzle Lord Bentley.

Aunt Rebecca and Harriet had to survive on a tiny annuity. Under the terms of the late Mrs. Clifton's will, Pringle House could not be sold, or they would forfeit their annuity. Mrs. Clifton had gone to her grave convinced that everything would turn out splendidly for her daughters. Having never handled any money or bills herself, she was sure the annuity would be ample enough to keep the large house and large staff. The clause forbidding the sale of Pringle House had been put there for sentimental reasons. Mrs. Clifton had loved the mansion and wished it to stay in the Clifton family.

''When did we last write to Cordelia?'' asked Harriet suddenly.

''On her birthday, last June. We always send her a little present on her birthday.''

''And she did not even bother to reply,'' said Harriet grimly, ''although that shawl you crocheted took months, and the silks cost us more than we could really afford.'' Harriet took a sustaining gulp of port.

The kitchen fire crackled busily as the wind outside began to rise and snowflakes whispered against the windows.

Harriet took a deep breath. ''I think, Aunt,'' she said, ''that we should pay Cordelia a visit.''

''Just what I was thinking,'' said Aunt Rebecca calmly, much to Harriet's surprise, since she had braced herself to face another bout of hysterics. ''I was much taken with the Marquess of Arden,'' went on Aunt Rebecca, knitting busily. ''Such a fine man. And not at all old. About thirty, I should think. The gentlemen, *both* of them, were attracted to you, dear Harriet.''

''Mr. Hudson was in his altitudes, and the marquess did not favor me at all, although I must allow his manners were of the best,'' added Harriet with feeling, remembering how carefully he had kept silent over having seen her naked.

''But he is only *one* man,'' said Aunt Rebecca dreamily. ''When the Season comes, London will be full of them just waiting to be picked up, like pebbles.''

''I was not thinking of marriage,'' said Harriet. ''I was thinking of warmth and comfort and food. If Cordelia thought she did not have to show me to her friends, but simply feed me, I do not think she would mind so much.''

''Our yearly allowance is due next week,'' said Aunt Rebecca. ''It is not much, and we cannot possibly spend it all or we would have no money for our return. But perhaps we might have enough to purchase two outside seats on the stage.''

"I could sell the hens to Farmer Pennyfeather," said Harriet, "and leave the keys of the house with the church for safekeeping. It is not as if we have to worry about being robbed. We have nothing left to steal." She giggled. "Won't Cordelia be furious!"

"No, no. I am sure her natural good feelings, which have long lain dormant, will come to the surface," said Aunt Rebecca. "I will write to her tomorrow and apprise her of our coming."

"No, don't do that," said Harriet slowly. "We'll surprise her."

"Oh, yes," said Aunt Rebecca, smiling through a rosy, port-induced mist. "That *will* be fun!"

Chapter Two

When the next morning dawned, cold and sleety, Aunt Rebecca had become nervous and anxious again. The idea of packing up and journeying to London to throw themselves on Cordelia's hospitality seemed a terrifying idea in the sober light of day.

Aunt Rebecca pottered miserably and uselessly about the kitchen and then announced she was taking to her bed for the rest of the morning because all the excitement of the day before had badly damaged her nerves.

Harriet was forced to confess to herself that she did not feel very courageous either, but there were the seemingly endless household chores induced by poverty and lack of servants to keep her busy.

It was only when she found herself looking for an old pair of cotton gloves to cover her hands, which she had just anointed in a mixture of bacon grease and lemon juice to reduce their redness, that she realized she was still determined to go to London, and repairing her damaged hands was one little step in that direction.

By early afternoon, wails and shuffling sounds from Aunt Rebecca's bedroom, which was in the old study off the hall, heralded her second appearance of the day.

Then came the clamor of the door knocker.

Harriet ran to answer the door, her heart beating hard.

A liveried servant stood on the steps. "The Marquess of Arden's compliments," he said. "Will you deliver this package to Miss Harriet Clifton direct? His lordship said it was most important."

Harriet realized he took her for the maid, but did not correct him. She could hardly wait until she had regained the kitchen so that she could open the small parcel.

Aunt Rebecca came in as she was tearing off the paper.

"Was that someone at the door, my love?" she asked.

"A servant with this package from the Marquess of Arden," Harriet told her.

Harriet ripped off the last piece of paper and looked in dismay at a small, square morocco jewel box. He could not possibly be sending her jewelry. Gentlemen did not send jewelry to young misses unless they were members of the Fashionable Impure. Perhaps he thought she was!

She opened the box and lifted out a letter that was lying on top. Underneath, embedded in silk, were ten golden sovereigns.

"Dear Miss Clifton," she read. "Pray accept this small payment to compensate for the murder of your birds. On behalf of myself and my cousin, I wish to thank you and your aunt for a most pleasant impromptu visit. Yr. Humble Servant, Arden."

She read it again, aloud.

"Ten sovereigns!" exclaimed Aunt Rebecca. "And presented with such tact." She sat down in a chair and rested her chin on her hand and thought hard.

The Marquess of Arden was unmarried. He had gone to extraordinary lengths to be kind to them. Correction. To be kind to *Harriet*. Therefore, it followed he had been struck by her beauty. Aunt Rebecca adored romances. Gentlemen were always being "struck" by beauty. It would be wicked—it would be flying in the face of providence—not to take Harriet to London.

Aunt Rebecca wandered off into a comfortable dream where Harriet was the Marchioness of Arden, and she herself, dressed in the finest silk and covered with a Norfolk shawl, held court in the fashionable West End of London.

"What are you thinking?" asked Harriet.

"I am thinking," said Aunt Rebecca slowly, "that we have a great deal to do before we go to London."

Harriet gave her a quick hug. "So we *are* going! What *will* Cordelia say, I wonder?"

"She cannot turn us away," said Aunt Rebecca stoutly.

Cordelia Bentley had a strong and healthy constitution, which was just as well since the latest fashions were causing the fair sex to drop like flies from pneumonia and influenza.

Despite the chill spring, Cordelia was dressed to receive visitors in a gown of thinnest pink India muslin, long pink gloves, heelless slippers, a white slip, and nothing else.

Her golden hair was cut fashionably short and formed a tight cap of curls on her small head.

She had wide blue eyes, a neat, straight nose, and a small, full-lipped, pouting mouth. By keeping to a rigorous diet prescribed by that leader of fashion Beau

Brummell—vinegar and boiled potatoes—she had managed to combat a tendency to run to fat.

She had shrewdly invested the money she had gained from the sale of the Bentley estates in the Funds and was therefore able to keep a smart house on Hill Street in Mayfair, and a staff of well-trained servants and to look about for a new husband at her leisure.

She had had two discreet affairs since the death of her husband, both of which had augmented her bank balance. But fear of losing respectability and therefore spoiling her chances of a successful marriage had rendered her celibate. She was determined to become the Marchioness of Arden, although she feared Lord Arden did not have marriage in mind. Still, she was confident of bringing him to heel and dragging him to the altar. The power of her beauty had grown, and at twenty-five, she knew she outshone any of the new and younger beauties on the London scene.

Her house was furnished in the latest fashion. Everything was in gold and red stripes. In her drawing room was a very fine portrait of herself and Harriet when they were children, painted by Sir Thomas Lawrence. She had told Aunt Rebecca and Harriet that she had sold it, but, in fact, she had decided to keep it to provide herself with evidence of an aristocratic background.

Guests admired it greatly and listened with rapt attention when she told the sad story of her baby sister, Harriet, who had died in her arms on the riverbank after she, Cordelia, had bravely tried to rescue her from drowning. Cordelia had told the story so many times she had quite come to believe it herself.

She was sure it had impressed the Marquess of Arden. Certainly, his surly cousin, Mr. Hudson, had looked upon her with rare enthusiasm and, the last time he had called, had asked her to repeat the story.

Cordelia was expecting the marquess to call. She hoped he would come alone instead of bringing that awful cousin with him as he usually did.

She rang the bell and told the butler to tell Mrs. Hurlingham to present herself in the drawing room.

Cordelia did not like Mrs. Hurlingham, but she paid her nonetheless for her services as a companion.

She had found that a young widow needed the company of a respectable female to give her ton. She had placed a discreet advertisement in the *Morning Post* and had hired a hotel room for the day in which to interview the applicants, not wishing to cope with a line of dull females in her own home.

Agnes Hurlingham proved to be exactly the sort of female Cordelia felt she required. Mrs. Hurlingham had never been married but had simply adopted the title of a married woman when she had reached the great age of thirty. She was now thirty-one. She was a short, heavy-set woman with a heavy, sallow face from which two small bright blue eyes burned with the grim light of sexual frustration, combined with all the other frustrations imposed on a highly intelligent, passionate woman of insufficient education who had been confined in a narrow cell of country life and genteel poverty.

She was a bishop's daughter, and the one thing she had in common with Cordelia was that her father had been a spendthrift during his lifetime and had died leaving his only daughter in straitened circumstances.

But she hailed from the untitled aristocracy, and every dowdy line of her breathed gentility, respectability, and breeding. Agnes Hurlingham did not like Cordelia, but she was grateful to her for all the comforts of a home in the West End, and of the two of them she was the one who enjoyed the plays and operas—

unlike Cordelia, who judged the evening by the notables in the audience.

Agnes's duties were to act as companion and chaperone. With her present, Cordelia felt that she had license to flirt outrageously. No one could accuse her of being *fast* with such a dragon beside her.

Agnes walked into the drawing room and slumped down in her usual chair well away from the fire. She was wearing a dowdy gown of some repellent brown stuff that seemed to be held together at the neck by a large mourning brooch.

"Who have we today, Lady Bentley?" she asked. "Arden, I suppose."

"Yes, Arden, and let us hope he leaves his cousin behind. It is very hard to indulge in dalliance with that young man glooming and dooming around the place."

"He is young, younger than you," said Agnes, taking out some dingy gray knitting from a workbasket.

"Youth is no excuse for bad manners. Don't slouch, Agnes."

Agnes straightened her spine and stabbed one long needle into the gray wool on her lap as if she wished it were Lady Bentley's cold heart.

Cordelia heard the ponderous steps of her butler, Findlater, approaching the drawing room and hissed, "He is come. He is arrived."

She ran to the mirror and patted a curl into place.

"A Miss Rebecca Clifton and a Miss Harriet Clifton," announced Findlater.

Lady Bentley's pretty shoulders stiffened, but she did not turn around.

"Tell them," she said clearly, "we are not at home."

Harriet and Aunt Rebecca had had an exhausting time of it reaching London. Some young blood up on the roof had decided to try his hand with the ribbons and had ended up overturning the stage into a ditch. They and the other passengers were bruised and shaken but mercifully escaped worse hurt. But it had taken ages for the substitute coach to arrive. They had been unable to book rooms at the nearest inn, due to lack of money, and had had to spend an uncomfortable night dozing on chairs in the inn parlor.

Their companions on the journey—three young bloods, a farmer's wife, a clerk, and a maidservant—had all become rather tipsy and loud at the inn, and familiarity with these new acquaintances made Harriet long to see the last of them.

When they were finally set down in the City, they had great difficulty finding a hack to take them to the West End. It was the busiest time of the day. Postmen in scarlet coats with bells were going from door to door. Bakers were shouting, "Hot loaves!" Chimney sweeps with brushes, hawkers with bandboxes on poles, milkmaids with manure on their feet and pails suspended from yokes across their shoulders were all crying their wares, competing with the bells of dust carts and the horns of news vendors. Great brewer's sledges pulled by enormous horses rumbled across the cobbles. At last an elderly gentleman took pity on them and engaged a hack. The jehu brightened at the fashionable address, but only the imposing figure of a liveried footman on the steps of Cordelia's house on Hill Street stopped the disappointed driver from cursing his fare over the paucity of the tip.

Both Harriet and Aunt Rebecca were dressed in black silk, since black silk had been a "special" at the mercer's in Lower Maxton. Aunt Rebecca had decided to add some color by fashioning herself a bonnet out of hen feathers and by draping her ample form with a multitude of colored scarves and shawls.

Harriet was wearing a bonnet of chip straw that was tolerably smart. It had been presented to her by the vicar's wife, who had social aspirations and had been much impressed by Harriet's grand statement that she was to have a season in London. Around her shoulders she wore a gold brocade stole, one of the few pretty relics of her mother's wardrobe.

Harriet had thought they both looked very fine when they set out from Pringle House. But here, in the heart of fashionable Mayfair, contrasting their clothes with the finery they saw about them, she feared they looked like a couple of upper servants trying without success to ape their betters.

She wanted to turn and flee. But the footman was stolidly waiting on the doorstep.

They had not been able to afford the expense of visiting cards, but Harriet had neatly penned their names on two homemade squares of card and had turned them down at the corners to show Cordelia that they were calling in person.

The footman gingerly took the cards and went back inside, shutting the door in their faces—an open condemnation of their shabby appearance.

At last, the door was opened again, this time by the butler, Findlater. He surveyed them sorrowfully, as if dealing with such persons went right to his heart, and inclined his head as a signal that they were to enter.

The hall was bright with flowers in vases and had a black-and-white tiled floor. A graceful staircase led to the upper floors.

"Please wait here," said Findlater grandly, and then proceeded to mount the staircase with maddening slowness.

"Well, here we are, Aunt Rebecca," said Harriet brightly.

"I wish we had not come," whispered Aunt Rebecca nervously. "The atmosphere of this house is *not* welcoming."

"Fustian," said Harriet bracingly. "I shall enjoy living here, I think."

Findlater came majestically down the stairs, their two cards on a silver salver. He fixed his eyes on the cornice. "My lady is not at home."

"What!" Harriet gasped. Then she recovered. "How silly of me. She has merely gone out." She looked hopefully at the butler. "We will wait until her return."

"That," said Findlater impassively, "would not be advisable."

Tears gushed out of Aunt Rebecca's eyes. "To refuse to see her own sister," she wailed. "It is too much. Oh, Harriet, I *cannot* go back in that coach again. I would rather *die*."

"At least we do have a home to go to," said Harriet gently, although her mind was working feverishly. The marquess's generosity had meant they had been able to travel inside, but now they had only enough money left to take two outside places.

"Come, Aunt," urged Harriet. "We are not wanted here."

There was a brisk knocking at the door.

Findlater opened it and bowed low before the two men on the step. "This way, my lord, Mr. Hudson," he said. "My lady is expecting you."

"Miss Harriet!" exclaimed Mr. Hudson, walking into the hall. "And Miss Clifton. What are you doing here?"

The Marquess of Arden stood framed in the doorway.

"We are just leaving," said Harriet in what she hoped was a dignified manner.

But at the sight of Mr. Bertram Hudson and the Marquess of Arden, Aunt Rebecca began to cry noisily again.

"It's so terrible," she said. "Cordelia will not even see us. Her own sister! And me . . . her aunt!"

"Her sister!" exclaimed Mr. Hudson. "But Lady Bentley said that her sister had died after she rescued her from the river."

"Are you Lady Bentley's sister?" demanded the marquess, his eyes fastened on Harriet's face.

"Yes," said Harriet stiffly. "Now, if you will excuse us . . ."

"No, we will not," said Mr. Hudson hotly. "If Lady Bentley ain't going to entertain you, then she ain't going to entertain *us*."

"What is all this commotion?" Cordelia appeared at the top of the stairs. Her blue eyes widened as she took in the scene: the marquess looking amused, Mr. Hudson glaring up at her in a fury, Aunt Rebecca weeping, and Harriet staring defiantly.

"I am sure Lady Bentley did not receive the message correctly," said the marquess. "Such a fair angel would not turn her own sister away."

"Harriet!" cried Cordelia. "Is it really you? *Stoopid* man, Findlater. I thought you said Crampton."

She ran lightly down the stairs and gave Harriet an affectionate hug.

Then she swung around gaily and smiled bewitchingly up at the marquess. "Here is my little mouse of a sister come from the country. You naughty child, Harriet. You should have apprised me of your arrival. What brings you to town?"

"To stay with you," said Harriet, eyeing her sister cynically.

For one brief moment, Cordelia's beautiful eyes went hard and cold.

"But we cannot stand here in the hall," she said, rallying. "Come upstairs to the drawing room."

Once in the drawing room, Cordelia ignored Agnes, who was standing, obviously waiting to be introduced, and drew Aunt Rebecca to a sofa by the fire. Her mind was working furiously. Once the marquess left, she could send her sister and aunt packing.

Harriet stood looking toward Agnes. "You have not introduced us to this lady."

She admired the delicate pink that rose to Cordelia's cheeks. Now, when I am annoyed, thought Harriet, I go as red as a beetroot.

Cordelia performed the introductions. "Your sister!" exclaimed Agnes. Her eyes swiveled to the portrait. "But I thought . . ."

"What a fusspot you are, Agnes." Cordelia laughed. "Always thinking the most incoherent thoughts." She turned to the marquess. "Never tell me you have already met my little sister."

"I have had that pleasure," said the marquess. "We called at Pringle House when we lost our way."

"Goodness," said Cordelia. "You must have found it a sad mess." She waggled a playful finger at Harriet. "You and Aunt Rebecca are so miserly. . . ."

"On the contrary, dear sister," said Harriet in a flat voice, "you know we have barely enough to live on—hence our visit to you."

Cordelia's thin eyebrows vanished under her hairline. "Am I to take it," she said in a silky voice, "that you have *really* come to stay?"

"Yes," said Harriet stoutly. "Our trunks are in the hall."

Turning her back on the marquess and Mr. Hudson, Cordelia silently mouthed, "Oh, no, you don't."

"Famous!" exclaimed Mr. Hudson. "You will be a welcome addition to this Season's beauties, Miss Harriet."

The marquess looked from Cordelia's flushed face to Harriet's mutinous one and drawled, "Indeed, Lady Bentley, your beauty is heightened by your magnaminity. It is not every reigning belle who would welcome her little sister at the beginning of the Season. When hospitality and kindness are added to beauty, I find the sum total most . . . seductive."

"Why, I never *thought* of turning away dear Harriet or Aunt Rebecca. I quite *dote* on them," said Cordelia with a charming smile. "Dear, dear Harriet, you must be exhausted after your journey." Cordelia rang the bell. When Findlater appeared, she tripped lightly over to the door and murmured something in his august ear. Findlater inclined his head and replied in a low voice.

"Splendid!" said Cordelia, swinging about and clapping her hands. "Your rooms are ready and you may *both* retire. Agnes, do go with them. I am sure Mr. Hudson will be a most splendid chaperon."

"I had hoped for a little conversation with Miss Harriet," said Mr. Hudson stiffly.

"You will have plenty of chances in the weeks to come. Agnes!" Cordelia's lilting voice held a note of steel.

Harriet curtsied to the marquess and then to Mr. Hudson. Cordelia had already turned away and was bending over the teapoy, extracting canisters of tea. The graceful curve of her body thrust her breasts against the thin fabric of her gown. Harriet glanced at the marquess and noticed a yellow, predatory light in his hooded eyes as he looked at Cordelia. She felt a pang of disappointment. She had thought of him often since his visit to Pringle House. As time had gone by, she had begun to picture him as a noble and generous hero, the type of man who would be above her sister's petty wiles. But he had just proved to be like all the rest. And what Cordelia wanted, Cordelia always got.

Harriet gave a little sigh and followed Aunt Rebecca and Agnes from the drawing room.

The rooms allocated to them were an insult: two poky little chambers on the top floor, each sparsely furnished. Agnes's face was a careful blank.

"This is to be your sitting room, I believe," intoned Findlater, leading the way along a low-ceilinged corridor.

The room he ushered them into was little better than their bedchambers. It had obviously been a schoolroom once. A battered spinet stood in one corner, and a pile of slates lay on a chipped and scarred table. A large rocking horse stared glassily at them from beside the empty hearth. There was an odd assortment of furniture that had found its way up to the schoolroom when its use downstairs had been over. The room was very cold.

"We would like fires lit in *all* our rooms," said Harriet in a thin, little voice.

Findlater opened his mouth to say that he had been given no such orders, but there was something in the proud tilt of Harriet's little chin that silenced him.

"Well, here we are," said Aunt Rebecca brightly when the silent Agnes had left, followed by the butler. "At least Cordelia has welcomed us."

"She did not welcome us *at all*," said Harriet furiously. "She would have thrown us out had it not been for the opportune arrival of the Marquess of Arden and his cousin. She is as hard-hearted and selfish as ever she was. But beggars cannot be choosers. At least we are in London. I will talk to Cordelia about her shabby treatment when we see her at supper.''

But they were not to see Cordelia. It transpired that all their meals were to be served to them in the schoolroom.

''I don't care,'' said Harriet as they prepared for bed after having hung their meager stock of clothes away. ''I just don't *care*.''

But she cried herself to sleep, because the Marquess of Arden had not shown the slightest flicker of interest in her and because all her hopes that Cordelia might have changed had been dashed.

In the days that followed, Harriet and Aunt Rebecca were given to understand by a tight-lipped and embarrassed Agnes that Cordelia did not wish to see them belowstairs.

She had agreed to feed them and give them house room provided they kept out of the way. If either of them made a nuisance of herself, they would be turned out.

At first it was hard to bear. It was hard to sit at the window and watch Cordelia, dressed in an array of bewitching gowns, going out to balls and parties or for drives in the park with the Marquess of Arden.

If he or Mr. Hudson had asked to see me, thought Harriet sadly, Cordelia would have *had* to ask us downstairs.

Despite her initial brave front, Harriet was, in truth, afraid of her sister. She desperately did not want to be sent away before she and Aunt Rebecca had had some respite from the drudgery and poverty of Pringle House. Time and again she berated herself for her lack of spirit. Time and again she set out to descend the stairs to the drawing room to confront Cordelia. And time and

again she was forced to admit to herself that she lacked
the necessary courage.

The servants treated her with thinly veiled insolence
but were too unsure of her exact status in the household
to stint on either food or coals.

Harriet tried to count her blessings. They had food
and warmth. London lay before them. They had no
money, but at least they could venture out and go for
walks in the parks and look at the shops.

But Aunt Rebecca felt the humiliation of their situation keenly and indulged her "delicate nerves" to the
hilt, depressing Harriet by constant complaining until
Harriet could only be relieved when Aunt Rebecca took
to her bed.

And so Harriet, a lonely little figure, often went out
on her own, walking miles through the streets and
parks, trying to exhaust herself, to walk away all the
bitterness she felt for her sister.

Things were made harder for her because her conscience told her they had no right to expect more from
Cordelia.

Very early one morning, the Marquess of Arden,
who was exercising his horse in Rotten Row, saw
Harriet's small figure striding along under the trees of
Hyde Park.

He reined in his mount and swept off his hat. "Good
day to you, Miss Harriet," he said, swinging himself
down lightly from the saddle.

Harriet was so disenchanted with him, that she was
almost surprised his feet of clay did not make a clatter-
ing sound as he landed on the ground.

"Good day, my lord," she said stiffly.

"I am disappointed not to have seen you about," he
said, his eyes narrowing as he surveyed her shabby

appearance. "Lady Bentley tells me you do not enjoy balls or parties. I did not know you were a bluestocking."

"I did not know it either," said Harriet dryly, turning on her heel and beginning to walk away. He fell into step beside her, leading his horse.

"You should not be out walking without a servant," he said.

"It is early," said Harriet repressively. "There is usually no one about at this unfashionable hour."

The blue sky arched above, and a blackbird in a tree above their heads sent down a liquid cascade of sound.

Harriet glanced covertly at the marquess. He looked tall and powerful in a black coat, leather breeches, and top boots.

The marquess was studying Harriet, from her plain hat to her dowdy black silk dress covered by a shawl, to her worn half boots.

"It is still quite cold in the early mornings," he said. "Have you nothing warmer to wear?"

"You forget," said Harriet. "I am used to the cold."

"Are you in mourning?"

"No, my lord," said Harriet, exasperated. "Black silk was a good bargain at the local shop."

"Mr. Hudson and I inquired after you several times, but we were always told you were gone from home."

"Indeed?" said Harriet, folding her lips into a thin line. She did not want to tell him Cordelia had lied. Like most besotted men, he would probably not believe a word against his beloved. On the other hand, if he did, he might tell his cousin, and that impassioned young man might tax Cordelia with it, and she and Aunt Rebecca would find themselves on the next stage-coach back to Pringle House.

Sometimes Harriet wondered why they did not just give up and leave. Things were not so bad in the country in the summer. There were plenty of vegetables, and she had kept one of her father's guns and sometimes went out on midnight hunting forays, knowing the locals would be shocked to learn that a lady was potting game, even on her own property.

The marquess studied her averted face, suddenly remembering what she had looked like naked. He felt his pulses quicken, and his mind firmly, with a great effort, banished the vision of a nude and rosy Harriet with water streaming down her body from his mind. The girl was undoubtedly a virgin, and a lady, although he was sure she would not long retain either virtue if she continued to live with her sister.

He was well aware that Cordelia was hard and selfish. He also knew her reputation and was anxious to bed her without the ties of marriage. He felt sure Cordelia's mercenary little heart would soon overcome her hopes of a respectable marriage, and he had dropped broad hints that he was prepared to be generous. His cousin Bertram had only lately come to town, having finished several undistinguished terms at Oxford University. Mrs. Hudson, his father's sister, was a widow and in poor health. She had begged the marquess to sponsor her son and to keep him out of the claws of card sharps, ivory turners, and the ladies of the town. The marquess found Bertram a tiresome young man, but he was fond of his aunt, so he took Bertram around with him as much as possible. Every time he went to Cordelia's drawing room, the marquess planned to leave Bertram behind, and yet every time he found himself taking the boy along. The marquess was looking for a mistress and had already decided on Cordelia, since he found her to be extremely beautiful and knew that the more mercenary the woman, the easier she was to get rid of once the affair began to pall. But there was always something at the back of his mind that stopped him from making Cordelia a firm, if disreputable, offer.

He was sorry for Harriet and annoyed with her at the same time. Since her arrival, Cordelia's character defects had begun to seem more glaring.

Harriet's black hair was now crammed up under a bonnet. He remembered how it had looked, cascading about her shoulders like a gleaming black river, when she sat at the spinet.

Harriet was recollecting his generous payment for the hens.

"I must thank you, my lord," she said, "for the ten sovereigns you sent me. It was more than the birds were worth."

"I think not," he said. "Two good laying hens obviously meant a lot to you."

"Thank you," said Harriet awkwardly. She wished he would go away. His very presence was disturbing her. He was a rake and no doubt felt obliged to charm every female he came across.

"I am giving a ball," he said. "An unusual thing for a gentleman to do, I admit. We usually leave all the entertaining of that nature to the ladies. But I am anxious to introduce Bertram to some respectable young company. There is nothing like an interest in the ladies to counteract the bad influence of the stables and gaming tables."

"I do not think you have to worry," said Harriet. "Mr. Hudson appears to be of a romantic disposition."

"Perhaps. I think it may be a pose to cover his shyness. If I sent you a card, would you come to my ball, Miss Harriet?"

"I will try," said Harriet. She had nothing to wear, but she was interested in a gloomy way to see if Cordelia would intercept the invitation. "When is it to be?"

"In a week's time. I had meant to send you an invitation, but I was becoming convinced of your aversion to frivolity."

"I would like to be frivolous . . . for a little," said Harriet. She looked so forlorn, he had an impulse to take her in his arms and kiss her, and was quite startled at the intensity of his own desire.

"Then I shall hope to see you, and your aunt, of course. May I escort you home?"

"You are very kind, my lord, but I would prefer to walk by myself for a little."

She curtsied to him gracefully and then moved quickly away across the grass. The marquess stayed, watching her slight figure in its ugly black dress until she was out of sight.

Harriet eventually made her way back to Hill Street, feeling shabby and depressed.

As she walked up past the drawing room, she could hear Cordelia's voice raised in anger. "Do you know what that *cat* Lady Jessop said to me t'other night, Agnes? She said, 'How clever of you to be able to bring your sister back to life. You must indeed be the enchantress all the gentlemen say you are.' "

"Shouldn't have told that tarradiddle about her drowning," said Agnes gruffly.

"I didn't say anything of the sort, and you know it," said Cordelia waspishly. "I don't know what everyone is talking about. I *never* said such a thing." Like all consummate liars, Cordelia was already beginning to believe she had never told that fairy story about trying to save her sister from drowning. "Harriet is a shabby embarrassment and *must* go. She and that old frump of an aunt have had time enough, sponging off me. You must tell them to leave, Agnes."

"Shouldn't you tell them yourself? She *is* your sister, you know."

"I pay you to do as you are told, so let me have none of your impertinence, Agnes. I am to go to the opera tonight. Get rid of them before I return. There is a stage leaving the White Hart at eight o'clock this evening. Make sure they are on it."

Harriet stood outside the door, shaking with rage. To be sent off to the country like an unwanted parcel! Cordelia would go to the marquess's ball, where she would lie and giggle about her little sister who preferred a life among the hayseeds to the sophistication of town. It was past bearing, but Harriet knew there was nothing she could do to stop them from being sent away.

All at once, she felt she had to get out of the house again, away from Cordelia's selfish malice, away from Aunt Rebecca's nerves, away from the insolent servants.

She had three shillings in her pocket, part of the very little money remaining of the marquess's generosity. If Cordelia wanted them to go, thought Harriet furiously, then she could pay for inside seats on the coach for them.

She decided to go out again, to walk until she was really tired and then treat herself to an ice at Gunter's, Gunter's being one of the very few places in London a lady could visit unaccompanied.

Out she went, along Hill Street, down Chesterfield Street, across Curzon Street, through Shepherd Market, and across Piccadilly into the quiet of Green Park, where tame deer came to nuzzle her hand.

Few of the fashionable crowd paid any attention to her, judging her to be a lady's maid by her sober blacks.

She walked and walked, now determined to stay away until that stagecoach had left. It was awful to think of going back to Pringle House, to a life of drudgery and poverty, before she had had any fun at all. Harriet was young and romantic. She longed for frivolity and pretty dresses. If Cordelia had been kind and had treated her to only a few weeks of the Season, Harriet felt sure she would have returned to the country content.

It was only the thought of Aunt Rebecca having to face dismissal on her own that made her think of turning her steps back toward Hill Street.

She had wandered as far as the City. The road back seemed very long. Her worn boots were beginning to hurt her feet. Her stomach rumbled with hunger. She had gone to Gunter's earlier, but the sight of all the fashionably dressed ladies and gentlemen eating ices inside had made her too shy to enter.

She walked down Oxford Street into Hanover Square and blinked at the commotion that met her eyes.

Chapter Three

Smoke was pouring from a tall building at the corner of the square.

As Harriet watched, a tongue of flame shot out from a downstairs window. She worked her way to the front of the crowd, praying that no one was trapped inside.

"Make way!" shouted a man. "Here comes the 'surance."

In fine style, the Reliable Insurance Fire Brigade rolled up to the front of the house, the bell clanging merrily.

The firemen were dressed in blue jackets, canvas trousers, and hardened leather helmets that had hollow leather crests over the crowns. This form of helmet, Harriet had read, was taken from the war helmet of the New Zealanders. It had the addition of a hind flap of leather to prevent burning matter from falling down the fireman's neck. The foreman wore his silver badge of office and carried a baton in one hand a leatherbound notebook in the other. He consulted the notebook as soon as he jumped down from the fire engine.

"Who lives here?" he demanded laconically as soot-blackened servants piled all the furniture and paintings they had been able to salvage in the square outside.

"My mistress," said a butler, gasping. "Her maid has just told us she was asleep when the fire broke out and she had locked herself in her room. She is the Dowager Duchess of Macham. We've got to rescue her."

"Let me see," said the foreman, thumbing the pages of his book. "Lindsey, Longham, Lumley . . . Ah, Macham. Ain't paid her insurance this age. Come along, boys. No pay, no service."

An elderly lady appeared at one of the upper windows, screaming for help.

"You can't go," said Harriet, catching the foreman by the sleeve. "In the name of humanity, you cannot leave her to burn."

"She should've thought of that and paid up," said the foreman, shrugging Harriet off.

Harriet looked about desperately. A fireman had left a leather bucket of water at the side of the pavement.

She sprang into action. Seizing the bucket, she doused herself from head to foot with the contents and, without pausing to think of the danger, ran headlong into the burning house.

"What's happening?" cried a Mr. Harry Postlethwaite, one of London's latest ornaments and a Pink of the Ton, scrambling up on top of a carriage to join his friends. "Can't see a demned thing."

"Some gel's run right into the building," said one of his friends. "Gone to rescue that old duchess creature, Macham."

"By jove," said Mr. Postlethwaite. "More over there,

chaps, and let me see. Gad's 'oonds! What a sight. It's better than Astley's. I say,'' he added recklessly. "I'll lay you a monkey that gel gets her out.''

His friends eagerly began to lay bets and their gambling fever spread to the crowds around, although his faith in Harriet was not shared. It was ten to one that the dowager would burn.

The fire had miraculously not yet reached the staircase. Harriet sprinted up the steps two at a time and hurtled along the upper corridor that led to the bedchambers, flinging open door after door, until she finally crashed into the Dowager Duchess of Macham's bedroom, gasping as the acrid smoke went down into her lungs. Why the duchess, who had unlocked her door too late to be assisted by her servants, should not have tried to escape by the way in which Harriet had come, instead of screaming for help from the window, was a mystery. The shock of her predicament, combined with the fumes, had overpowered her, and the duchess lay by the window, a crumpled and unconscious figure.

Harriet's years of chopping wood, carrying pails of water from the pump, and scrubbing floors stood her in good stead. She slung the frail body of the duchess easily over one shoulder and ran for the door, only to retreat back into the room with a cry of dismay. The end of the corridor at the upper landing was now a blazing inferno.

She set the duchess down and leaned out of the window. A hoarse cheer went up from the crowd below.

Harriet twisted her neck and looked up. There was only one more floor before the roof and a thick drainpipe ran up beside the window.

She tore off her crumpled bonnet and hitched her long, still damp skirts up by the tucking folds of the clinging black material into the tapes of her gown. Kicking off her boots, she picked up the duchess again and edged out onto the sill until she was standing there above the roaring crowd with the duchess over her shoulder.

Thanking God that her grace weighed little more than a child, Harriet gripped the drainpipe firmly in both hands and began a lopsided climb, praying that the duchess would not recover consciousness and struggle, since she needed both hands free.

The crackling and roaring of the fire eating at the building lent her the strength of a madwoman. Up she went, inching her way, the limp figure of the old woman hanging like a sack over her shoulder.

A silence fell on the watching crowd below, a silence broken only by the petulant voice of Mr. Bertram Hudson demanding loudly from the edge of the square, "What is going on?"

"Quiet," said the Marquess of Arden. His great height allowed him to see above the heads of the crowd.

Normally, the square would have been dark, lit only by the flickering, feeble lights of the parish lamps. But the raging blaze from the building threw everything into high relief: the gaping crowd, the jostling hawkers selling gingerbread and hot chestnuts as if at a fair, and the slim, black figure edging up to the roof, the body on her shoulder.

Pray God, she makes it, thought the marquess. Can it possibly be Miss Harriet? Or am I being haunted by slim girls dressed in black silk?

A sudden desperate urge to do something, anything, to help that gallant little figure made him begin to shoulder his way through the crowd with Bertram Hudson following behind, still querulously demanding to be told what it was all about.

Harriet felt herself becoming giddy and faint. The gutter was just above her head, but all at once the madness of fear that had given her strength left her.

A sigh like the wind passed through the watching crowd. It seemed certain she would fall.

The marquess groaned. The downstairs floors were a raging inferno. There seemed no way he could get to her.

''Go on!'' he shouted suddenly. ''Go on, Harriet. You can make it.'' He was still not quite sure whether the slight figure now far above his head as he stood in front of the burning building *was* Harriet. But he called again, desperately, ''Go *on*. Climb!''

''Climb!'' roared the crowd, taking up her name. ''Climb, Harriet.''

Harriet clenched her teeth, taking courage from the noise below. She stretched up one hand to the gutter.

The duchess moaned and stirred.

''Don't,'' pleaded Harriet. ''Don't move.'' She needed both hands to climb up onto the roof, and so long as the duchess remained a limp, inert figure, it was possible. She could not manage it if she had to stop to hold on to a frightened woman.

The duchess mercifully swooned again.

Harriet's toe found a good-sized crack in the side of the building. Above the gutter was a low balustrade, and behind that a small space between the balustrade and the steep slope of the tiled roof.

With a superhuman effort, her muscles cracking, she heaved herself up and over, she and the duchess tumbling over the balustrade to lie facedown on the other side.

The wild cheering of the crowd was suddenly stilled as a great tongue of flame broke through the roof several yards to the left of where Harriet was lying.

Harriet struggled to her feet, picked up the duchess in her arms, and set off in a shambling run along the edge of the roof toward the adjoining building.

At the edge of the roof she stopped in dismay. There was a gap of twelve feet to the next building. She could not possibly jump it with the old woman in her arms.

Behind her came a terrible rumble and crash as part of the roof fell in.

The heat of the roof under her feet was becoming intense. Down below a sea of white faces stared up.

"Help!" cried Harriet piteously. "Help!" But her voice was drowned by the roaring and crackling of the fire.

And then she heard her name.

"Harriet," said an imperative voice. "Over here. Move quickly."

The Marquess of Arden was standing on the other roof, untying a stout length of rope from about his waist.

"I will throw you one end," he called. "Tie it firmly to the parapet."

The rope snaked over. Harriet laid the duchess gently against the slope of the roof and seized the rope. At first her hands were trembling too much to tie it securely, but at last she managed to knot it firmly.

The marquess, who had secured his end, stripped off his coat, kicked off his boots, and made his way, hand over hand, across the intervening gap.

"Come along, Miss Harriet," he said. "Your troubles are over."

"Take her first," said Harriet, gasping, pointing to the duchess.

"Very well. I will be as quick as I can. Pray God you do not lose your life in this rescue of one of London's most parsimonious, selfish old hags." He unwound a thinner length of rope from his waist. "Tie her on my back. Hurry!"

The duchess was lashed to his back. He crossed quickly to the other roof, slashed at the rope that bound the duchess to him with a knife, and tumbled her unceremoniously onto the tiles.

He swung himself back over again and seized Harriet. "Put your arms about my neck," he said urgently.

"I can't," said Harriet, trembling. Her legs seemed to have turned to water and her arms to have lost their strength.

He bent his head suddenly and kissed her full on the lips, a hard, intense kiss.

Then he looked down at her, his eyes glinting in the red light from the fire. "Please do not be missish, Harriet," he said severely.

"Missish!" Harriet gasped, and then she began to giggle.

"That's better. Hold on to me."

Harriet put her arms tightly about his neck. She could feel his muscles rippling under his shirt as he swung down onto the rope, with her tightly pressed against his back.

With a shattering roar the roof behind them gave way, a huge pillar of flame shot up, scorching loose the end of the rope that Harriet had tied to the parapet, and they plunged down into the space between the houses. The marquess braced his feet to take the impact as they struck the opposite building.

Then he began to climb up. White-faced, Harriet clung to him.

He climbed quickly and nimbly up onto the other roof and set Harriet on her feet.

Down below, the crowd cheered themselves hoarse. The marquess looked down at Harriet. Her gown had dried but was ripped and torn. There was a smudge of soot on her left cheekbone and a scratch on her right. Her hair was a wild and tangled mess. Her eyes, looking up into his face, seemed enormous.

He gathered her into his arms and kissed her very gently this time. Harriet closed her eyes. She could hear the roar of the crowd and the greedy crackling of the fire, she could feel her breast being crushed against his chest, and then suddenly all she could feel were his lips moving against her own. The world became dark and silent, an odd mixture of passion and peace.

"Disgraceful!" cackled a malicious old voice from somewhere at their feet. "Kissing and cuddling while I'm at death's door."

The marquess gently set Harriet away from him and looked down into the bright evil eyes of the Dowager Duchess of Macham.

"Oh, it's you, Arden." The duchess sniffed. "Might have known. Never could leave women alone. S'pose you rescued me."

"No," said the marquess. "You owe your life to Miss Clifton here."

"Her? S'pose she'll want money."

"No, she does not want money, you reprehensible old harridan. I wish you had not recovered your horrible senses so quickly," snapped the marquess. "If your old carcase has as much energy as your tongue, we can make our way out of this building before it catches fire as well."

"I am going to faint," said the little duchess, struggling to her feet.

"I do not care what you do," said the marquess nastily. "I am going to take Miss Clifton to safety."

"Ha! Take her to your bed, more like."

"If you, madam, take it upon yourself to broadcast

to the world that I gave Miss Clifton a chaste embrace, I will personally set you on fire."

"It ain't that I ain't grateful to her," whined the duchess. "You should take better care o'me, Arden, 'stead o' preachin' and moralizin'. The night air is cold."

"Then I suggest you warm yourself at your fire," said the marquess, jerking his thumb in the direction of the blazing building.

The duchess began to moan about the loss of her valuables. Harriet tried to reassure her by saying she had seen a great amount of furniture and paintings piled up outside on the street, but the marquess led her firmly away.

The building they descended into through a skylight had been evacuated, and with the little duchess grumbling behind them, they made their way down through the deserted rooms and passages.

The marquess put an arm around Harriet's shoulders as he led her out into the square. The noise and cheering of the crowd were deafening. They surged forward, threatening to crush her to death in their enthusiasm.

Mr. Hudson was there, plucking at Harriet's sleeve and babbling, "The bravest thing I ever saw. You should have told me what you meant to do, Arden. *I* would have rescued her. *I* . . ."

The marquess swung Harriet up into his arms and began to shoulder his way through the cheering crowd.

Cordelia was late for the opera. She was not much troubled by that fact, since she had no interest in the music, only in the effect caused by her appearance.

"Did you tell them?" she asked Agnes over her shoulder.

"Miss Harriet is gone from home and has not returned," said Agnes. "As for old Miss Clifton, she is not well, and I prefer to order her out when her niece is with her to sustain her. I will be able to accompany you after all."

Cordelia narrowed her eyes. "Be sure you have told them, one way or t'other by the time I return. You need not accompany me, Agnes," she added maliciously, knowing how much Agnes loved the opera.

"Don't like going in halfway through the opera anyway." Agnes shrugged, though her intense gaze bored into Cordelia's back as her young mistress turned back to the mirror. "Listen to that noise. It's coming closer. If the mob's out, you may not be able to go yourself."

"War riots." Cordelia sniffed contemptuously. "One never knows what to do . . . whether to be for or against."

The Tories were *for* the British war against Napoleon's armies in the Spanish Peninsula, the Whigs against.

Both political parties rented mobs. There was the antiwar mob and the prowar mob. A British victory could mean your windows were smashed in for not displaying candles all over the house and drawing back the curtains in celebration, and the antiwar mob would wreak havoc with equal enthusiasm on any house that seemed to support the campaign.

"Tell the servants to light all the candles," said Cordelia, "and listen hard. If they're antiwar, draw the curtains."

"They are cheering. It must be a victory," said Agnes.

"Look out of the window and make sure."

Agnes raised the window and leaned out.

After a few moments, she drew her head in and gazed at Cordelia in a dazed way.

"It's Arden," she said. "At the head of a cheering mob with Miss Harriet in his arms."

Cordelia elbowed her aside and thrust her head out.

"The deuce," she muttered.

She turned from the window and ran from the room and down the stairs.

The noise of cheering grew nearer and nearer.

Pinning a smile on her face, Cordelia opened the door.

The marquess was just setting Harriet down on her feet on the step.

"Dear me," said Cordelia. "Did little Harriet faint?"

"*Little* Harriet is a heroine," said Mr. Hudson. "She rushed into a burning building and saved the life of the Dowager Duchess of Macham."

"Poor Harriet," murmured Cordelia sweetly. "Always *so* impetuous."

The marquess gave her a cold look. Cordelia rallied and rushed forward and gathered Harriet in her arms.

"Come inside, dear," she cooed, "and we will put you to bed immediately. You must be *exhausted*."

"I confess I am a trifle tired," said Harriet with a watery smile.

"Agnes!" Cordelia called over her shoulder. "See Miss Harriet to her room."

"I will take my leave," said the marquess, looking down at Cordelia with an odd expression on his face.

Harriet was glad to escape out of range of Cordelia's gimlet eye. Harriet knew Cordelia was furious because she had once more brought herself to the Marquess of Arden's attention.

Aunt Rebecca was waiting at the top of the stairs, her large, moonlike face swimming in the gloom. She had heard the news of Harriet's bravery, as she, too, had leaned out of the window to watch her niece's triumphant arrival home. All the excitement had caused Aunt Rebecca to make one of her mercurial recoveries from nervous depression. Agnes led Harriet into the schoolroom and seated her by the fire, and then left Harriet to tell Aunt Rebecca about her adventures while Agnes went in search of brandy.

When she returned, she poured them all a strong measure.

"It seems you are the talk of London, Miss Harriet," said Agnes. "If you are not too exhausted, please tell me all about it. I have told the servants to carry a bath up to your bedchamber."

Harriet recited her tale of the fire and the rescue once more.

"But you are a heroine!" exclaimed Agnes. Then she fell silent, her intense gaze roaming around the shabby schoolroom while her mind worked busily.

Agnes was beginning to detest Cordelia. It was difficult, she thought, watching the candlelight flicker on Harriet's sensitive little face, to believe that two such sisters came out of the same stable.

Underneath her beauty, Cordelia was vulgar and coarse. Harriet, despite her shabby clothes and soot-stained face, still managed to look like the lady she was.

Agnes made up her mind. "I am going out for a little, Miss Harriet," she said. "I will return in time to see you before you go to sleep."

She left Aunt Rebecca and Harriet together and ran to fetch her cloak and bonnet. Then she called for a hack and set out in the direction of the City, calling at first one newspaper office and then the other.

Agnes Hurlingham knew Cordelia was hoping that Harriet's bravery would be quickly forgotten. And so Agnes was determined that the whole of London would know about the rescue of the duchess.

Meanwhile, as Harriet was enjoying a warm bath, Aunt Rebecca sat by the fire and turned over in her mind all Harriet had told her about the Marquess of Arden.

Aunt Rebecca felt ashamed of herself and what she considered her own abysmal lack of spirit. She should not have lurked in her room, frightened and depressed because Cordelia did not want them.

It was her God-given duty to see that Harriet found a husband. Mr. Bertram Hudson, for example, was certainly interested in Harriet. And perhaps the marquess himself would bear watching.

Taking advantage of the new deference of the servants, Aunt Rebecca rang for supper for herself and ordered a tray of delicacies to be offered to Harriet when she emerged from her bath.

As she had promised, Agnes returned in time to make sure Harriet was comfortably prepared for bed and had everything she needed.

Harriet smiled at her sleepily and said, "You are very kind to me, Mrs. Hurlingham. I cannot thank you enough."

Agnes's conscience smote her. She had only been kind to Harriet to spite Cordelia. "Call me Agnes," she said gruffly. "You should not really be in these quarters, you know. I will speak to Lady Bentley on the subject."

So it was that Cordelia, returning from the opera, found Agnes patiently waiting for her.

"Such devotion, Agnes," she said nastily, "or do you want to say something to add to my already disastrous evening? Society, I would have you know, was quite shocked to see me this evening. Why was I not at home tending to my brave little sister? Pah!"

"That is what I wanted to talk to you about," said

Agnes Hurlingham. "You're going to be in the suds unless you do something about her." She jerked her thumb inelegantly in the direction of the ceiling.

"Do something about Harriet?" demanded Cordelia with dangerous sweetness. "What *do* you mean, Agnes? I have already *told* you what has to be done with her. Send her packing."

"They'll be calling you a sort of Lady Macbeth if you do that to London's latest heroine," said Agnes. "They'll be calling in droves tomorrow just to get a look at her. And servants talk, you know. 'Fore you know it, it'll be 'round the ton that she and her aunt are housed in the attic. That her clothes are monstrous shabby. Ain't the conduct of a lady—*that's* what they'll say."

"Pooh!" said Cordelia. "No one will call. Furthermore, Agnes, I do not like your tone. Remember your place, my good woman. Call Martha and tell her to make me ready for bed. You silly woman! As if saving that old miser of a duchess that society has detested this age will make the slightest bit of difference!"

Agnes hardly slept that night. She was out in the street in the morning as soon as she heard the news vendor's horn, and, armed with all the papers, she retreated to her room. London in 1811 boasted eight morning papers. Agnes's large mouth widened into a grin of pleasure as she saw that every paper had given prominent space to the bravery of Harriet Clifton.

She rang for the butler and told him to make sure Lady Bentley was given the newspapers with her morning chocolate and then took herself off to bed. Only a month ago, on her birthday, Agnes had given way to a hearty bout of tears on seeing a life of servitude stretching out before her to the grave. For the first time in ages she began to feel that life might hold some interesting surprises. She smiled to herself as she fell asleep.

Harriet awoke to find the maids bustling about her room, packing up her meager belongings.

"What is happening?" she demanded, struggling awake.

"Lady Bentley's orders," said the housekeeper from the doorway. "We are to move you and Miss Clifton into rooms on the floor below. Lady Bentley's compliments and you are to present yourself in the drawing room, miss, at four o'clock. Her ladyship has supplied you with two gowns and begs you to pick whichever one you consider suitable." The housekeeper suddenly smiled. "It is so exciting, miss. The house is like a flower garden. Everyone in London seems to have sent presents and bouquets and poems. And the newspapers, Miss Harriet! Every single one has written about your bravery."

It was a bewildering day for Harriet. The new rooms allocated to her and Aunt Rebecca were elegantly furnished with a pretty, private sitting room between their two bedrooms.

Dressed in one of Cordelia's oldest gowns, a plain taffeta dress in half-mourning colors of dove gray piped with black that Cordelia had worn shortly after the death of Lord Bentley, Harriet sat in the drawing room, telling her story over and over again for the benefit of the ton.

Wrapped in her numerous shawls and scarves, Aunt Rebecca listened each time with the same enthusiasm with which she had heard the first account. Although Mr. Hudson was very much present, hanging onto Harriet's every word, the Marquess of Arden was not, and Aunt Rebecca felt a little pang of disappointment.

Cordelia smiled and smiled, feeling her face beginning to ache. She could not get rid of Harriet so long as this adulation lasted, and, worse, she was quite clearly expected to take Harriet with her to all the fashionable events of the Season.

Agnes Hurlingham's conscience troubled her. Her loyalty surely lay with the mistress who paid her wages, and not with these newcomers. She alone knew what it was costing Cordelia to smile and smile as tribute to her sister followed tribute.

But Agnes's pity for Cordelia was to be short-lived.

A soberly dressed gentleman introduced himself as Mr. Arthur Prenderbury and claimed to be a distant relation of the Cliftons. He was a scholarly-looking gentleman in his forties with a long, rather serious face and steady gray eyes. After having paid his compliments to Harriet, Cordelia, and Aunt Rebecca, Mr. Prenderbury seated himself next to Agnes and engaged her in conversation. Had she seen Mrs. Jordan in *Country Girl*? For his part he thought it a shocking mélange of absurdities.

Agnes began to talk about the theater, flattered by her companion's steady attention. He made her feel feminine and witty, and he laughed appreciatively at several of her sallies.

And then, "Mr. Prenderbury!" Cordelia sailed up, a vision in pale pink muslin embroidered with tiny rosebuds and a garland of silk rosebuds in her hair. "I have been sadly neglecting you. I see you have been keeping my poor old companion amused. Too kind. Do come and meet Lady Jenkins. She is quite a bluestocking and makes my poor head ache, since I have not the faintest notion of what she is talking about. But a scholar like you will be more than a match for her."

Mr. Prenderbury had risen to his feet as Cordelia had begun to speak. He hesitated, looking down at Agnes.

But Cordelia tucked her hand confidingly in his arm and gave him a blinding smile as he turned to say something to her. He blinked a little, like a man dazzled, and then moved away with her.

Agnes Hurlingham sat clenching and unclenching her fists. Greedy Cordelia! Mr. Prenderbury was the first man to appear in Cordelia's drawing room who had paid her, Agnes, the slightest bit of attention. But Cordelia had to have it all. Agnes longed to be able to walk out of the house in Hill Street and keep on walking, and to never see Cordelia again.

But Cordelia had made her sign a seven-year contract, a most odd arrangement for a lady's companion. If the contract was broken, then Agnes felt perfectly sure that Cordelia would enjoy taking her to court and ruining her.

She found herself joined by Aunt Rebecca. That lady plumped down amid a welter of scarves and shawls and trailing threads.

"I am so proud of Harriet," said Aunt Rebecca. "Her bravery has quite melted Cordelia's heart."

Agnes gave a grunt. Mr. Prenderbury was listening to Lady Jenkins. He did not laugh or smile at anything she was saying, and that gave Agnes an odd feeling of comfort.

"And to find a relative, too," enthused Aunt Rebecca, following Agnes's gaze. "Mr. Prenderbury *is* distantly related to us. The Prenderburys live in Suffolk. I remember hearing about Mr. Arthur Prenderbury from my late brother. He distinguished himself at Oxford as a young man. He is studying some manuscripts at the British Museum. He read all about Harriet in the newspapers."

"Indeed," said Agnes in a toneless voice. She took a deep breath and turned to Aunt Rebecca. "It is a pity the Marquess of Arden did not call. He appeared to be much taken with Miss Harriet.''

She had the satisfaction of seeing that she had Aunt Rebecca's full attention.

"But I was under the impression that Lord Arden was courting Cordelia.''

"No, no,'' said Agnes. "Lady Bentley is the fashion, that is all. Most of the gentlemen call regularly to pay court to her. It was fortunate that Lord Arden was on hand to assist Miss Harriet in her rescue of the duchess. That sort of adventure forms, er, a *bond*, don't you think?''

"Yes, I should imagine so,'' said Aunt Rebecca eagerly. "But Harriet has no dowry.''

"The Marquess of Arden is rich, *very* rich, and also very strong-willed. I do not think the little matter of an absence of dowry would deter him were his affections seriously engaged.''

At that moment, Mr. Prenderbury looked across the room and, catching Agnes's eye, smiled.

"I happen to know,'' Agnes went on smoothly after returning the smile, "that Lord Arden has sent invitations to a ball he is to give next week, one for you and one for Miss Harriet. They arrived early yesterday evening by hand.''

"How splendid!'' said Aunt Rebecca. Then her face dropped. "But Cordelia did not mention any invitations. Perhaps she may not tell us.''

"Oh, now that she is so proud of Miss Harriet, I am sure she will. But, to be diplomatic, one of Lord Arden's closest friends, Mr. Tommy Gresham, is here. Come with me and I will introduce you. That way you can tell Lady Bentley you learned of the invitations from *him*. That will jog her memory. She receives so many invitations, it would be quite like her to forget to pass on yours to you.''

Mr. Gresham was a large, fat, jovial man. With the ease of long practice in social situations, Agnes deftly separated him from a group of friends and introduced him to Aunt Rebecca.

''I was just telling Miss Clifton about Lord Arden sending invitations to his ball to her and Miss Harriet,'' said Agnes. ''I know Lord Arden is most anxious that Miss Harriet should attend. What is troubling Miss Clifton is that Lady Bentley has obviously forgotten to give her the invitations and she feels it would be rude to accuse her of a lapse of memory.''

His small blue eyes twinkling shrewdly in his large face, Mr. Tommy Gresham smiled. ''Oh, I'll remind her,'' he said cheerfully. ''Leave it to me. I'll say Arden told me to make sure Miss Harriet was coming.''

One fat eyelid drooped briefly in a wink before Mr. Gresham sailed off to talk to Cordelia.

Agnes saw Cordelia's face turn a delicate pink, and for a brief moment her expression was hard and ugly. Then she said something to Mr. Gresham, laughing and putting her hand on his sleeve.

Harriet was enjoying herself immensely. It was wonderful to be praised and admired. It was marvelous to be surrounded by people after having spent so much of her young life with only Aunt Rebecca for company.

She was relieved the Marquess of Arden was not present, or so she told herself. He was an uncomfortable sort of man.

For Harriet, the calls were over all too soon, and Cordelia was dismissing Aunt Rebecca and Agnes and demanding to see her *alone*.

''Well, sister,'' said Cordelia, leaning back in her chair and swinging one dainty foot, ''it appears you are the latest rage." She gave a delicate, catlike yawn. "Of course, it won't last. Next week it will be some actor or jockey or tattooed lady to take your place. But while it does it seems I must take you about with me. How fatiguing! I detest ingenues. Fortunately, I do not need to worry about your appearance outshining mine." Cordelia surveyed the demure figure in the gray and black gown opposite, failing to notice the beauty of her sister's eyes and hair. "Perhaps it will not be such a bad thing after all. Agnes is beginning to bore me. She can stay at home until all the furor about you dies down. You will need some gowns. Nothing too extravagant. I am not made of money. Martha can alter some of my old ones for you. There is just one little thing. . . ."

"Yes?" To her horror, Harriet felt that she was positively beginning to hate her own sister.

"There is the matter of Arden," said Cordelia. "I am hopeful of becoming a marchioness. You have drawn his attention to you in a way that displeases me. Make sure you do not do so again."

"On each occasion I met Lord Arden, it was by accident," said Harriet stiffly. "He called at Pringle House by chance and, also by chance, happened to be in Hanover Square at the time of the fire."

"Just make sure there are no other *chances*," said Cordelia. "*I* did not invite you or Aunt Rebecca, but I am prepared to tolerate you for a short length of time, provided you both behave yourselves."

"I am your sister," cried Harriet. "Surely there should be some natural spring of affection between us."

"Vastly touching, dear sis, but none on my side, I can assure you. *I* had to look after myself, and I suggest you learn to do the same."

"Marry some old man for his money?"

"Don't be impertinent, Harriet, or I shall slap your face. Just behave prettily and modestly, keep yourself in the background, and keep your eyes away from Arden, and we will rub along very well together. You will go to the marquess's ball. Should he ask you to dance, then you must refuse."

"But if I refuse Lord Arden," said Harriet, aghast, "then that means I cannot dance *at all*."

"Exactly. You and Aunt Rebecca may have the joy of watching the dancers. You expect too much for a little girl so recently come from the country. No, Harriet. You will do as you are bidden or I will send you home immediately."

When Harriet reached the seclusion of her bedchamber, she wondered why she had not told Cordelia she would not go to the ball. What was the point in attending if she could not dance?

The marquess's face swam before her mind's eye. She remembered all those delicious feelings she had experienced when he had kissed her. But she had never been kissed before. Therefore it followed she would experience the same sensations with another man.

Harriet then thought of Pringle House and of what her life had been there. It would be wonderful to be married and have a proper home. Perhaps some gentleman might be attracted to her during the Season, some man who would take all the cares and burdens of looking after herself and Aunt Rebecca from her shoulders.

Aunt Rebecca came shuffling in as Harriet was climbing into bed.

"What did Cordelia have to say?" she asked anxiously.

"Oh, provided I keep in the background and make

sure Lord Arden does not even look at me, we may stay for a little. She suggested I follow her example and entrap some old man.''

Aunt Rebecca sat down on the edge of the bed. ''There is young Mr. Hudson, Harriet.''

''I fear Lord Arden would have something to say about his young cousin proposing to a penniless girl.'' Harriet smiled. ''And think how exhausting it would be to be wed to such as Bertram Hudson. One would have to endure Gothic tragedies even at the breakfast table.''

''It is a pity about Arden,'' said Aunt Rebecca cautiously. ''I was sure he was not indifferent to you.''

''He has eyes only for such as Cordelia,'' said Harriet, primming her lips. ''I fear he regards all women as sluts. He—he kissed me, Aunt Rebecca.''

''Gracious! Where?''

''On the lips.''

''I mean, where did this happen?''

''On the roof, after he had rescued me and the duchess from the fire.''

''Well, the peril of the moment must have made him forget himself, for I am determined that Lord Arden is a fine gentleman in both rank and manner. Still, his behavior is very shocking, and had it happened in different circumstances, then he would be obliged to marry you. Perhaps it is my duty to call him to account for his behavior.''

''Oh, no, please, Aunt. We must have nothing to do wih him, or Cordelia will send us packing. Do you think we are behaving like weaklings, enduring her humiliating behavior just for a few balls and parties?''

''No, we have no choice.'' Harriet looked very small and childish as she lay against the pillows. ''But you may trust me to see to your future,'' said Aunt Rebecca. "*I* will take care of you to make up for all the times you have taken care of me and my poor nerves."

"Dear aunt." Harriet smiled. "Thank you."

But after Aunt Rebecca left, Harriet shook her head sadly.

What on earth could poor old Aunt Rebecca do?

Chapter Four

During the six days before the Marquess of Arden's ball, Harriet attended a few routs, one opera, and one musicale. Anxious for Aunt Rebecca's welfare and dreading the *crise de nerfs* that would undoubtedly be precipitated if they were given their marching orders, Harriet dutifully kept in the background.

She suspected the clothes that Cordelia had lent her were the most unbecoming her sister could find and that Cordelia had instructed her lady's maid, Martha, to take off all the becoming flounces, laces, and ornaments.

Little better dressed than Agnes, meek, and demure, Harriet played her part so well that by the day before the ball, society had largely forgotten about her and even Mr. Hudson no longer sought her company.

The Marquess of Arden was nowhere in sight, and his absence was making Cordelia dangerously petulant. Her scheme of punishing Agnes by leaving her at home had gone awry, as Cordelia discovered on returning

from an afternoon call with Harriet. She was told by
Findlater that Mrs. Hurlingham had gone out walking in
the park with Mr. Prenderbury.

Cordelia had thrown a famous tantrum, calling Agnes
a slut and forbidding Mr. Prenderbury the house. Harriet heard Agnes weeping during the night and had gone
to comfort her, but Agnes had screamed at her to go
away, saying she was only making matters worse.

And that was when Harriet decided that life at Pringle
House with all its attendant discomforts was infinitely
preferable to life with Cordelia.

She went back to her room and lit all the candles,
opened the wardrobe, and looked at the gown she was
meant to wear at the marquess's ball.

It was a skimpy affair of white muslin with a round
neck higher than was the current fashion and with little
puff sleeves. It had one flounce at the hem.

Behind it, swaying slightly in the draft, were the
other gowns Cordelia had lent her.

Harriet took out the ball gown and then two of the
other gowns, fetched her workbasket, and began to
work busily through the night.

The next evening, Agnes, still rather red about the
eyes, burst into Harriet's bedroom. "Lady Bentley is in
such a taking," she said, gasping. "She says you are
too late to go with us and must follow in a hack. Oh,
my dear, you look beautiful."

Harriet turned from the glass and smiled. The white
muslin gown now had a floating overdress of green
silk. The bosom was fashionably low, and a delicate
wreath of green silk flowers was entwined in her glossy
black hair. The remains of one of Cordelia's green silk
gowns lay on a chair.

"Very well," said Harriet. "Present my apologies to

Lady Bentley, Agnes, and tell her I will join her at the ball.''

Agnes hesitated. "Lady Bentley will not be pleased when she sees you, Harriet. You will outshine her."

"I have already decided to return to the country," said Harriet calmly, "so I do not care what she thinks."

"Agnes!" Cordelia screamed from downstairs.

"I must go," whispered Agnes. "Good luck!"

Harriet went into the sitting room, where Aunt Rebecca was patiently waiting for her.

"The plan worked," said Harriet. "She has gone off in the most awful miff."

"Oh, my dear," said Aunt Rebecca. "You look so very beautiful. What a pity . . ."

"Don't go on, Aunt. Confess that you yourself will be glad to be quit of here."

Aunt Rebecca looked mulish but did not say anything.

Resplendent in Weston's tailoring, the Marquess of Arden stood at the top of the graceful staircase in his town house in St. James's Square to receive his guests. Beside him, looking smaller and less sulky in formal evening wear, was Bertram Hudson.

The marquess was glad to notice that Bertram's enthusiasm for Harriet Clifton seemed to be on the wane. The conventional side of his character felt a certain distaste at the thought of any alliance with a family that contained Cordelia, Lady Bentley. The only trouble was that Harriet's sweetness and innocence had quenched his dishonorable intentions toward Cordelia. Besides, he preferred his mistresses to have no claims to respectability whatsoever.

He almost regretted his decision, however, as Cordelia floated up the staircase toward him in all the glory of gold tissue and blazing diamonds. She looked ethereally beautiful.

"Where is your sister, Lady Bentley?" he asked as she curtsied before him.

"La! She will soon be here, if she comes at all." Cordelia laughed. "I left her to make her own way. She is such a goose. So vulgar to be late," said Cordelia, who was rarely on time for anything herself and had only made a special effort because she was worried by the recent coolness of the marquess.

Agnes made her curtsy as well and followed Cordelia into the ballroom. Agnes saw Mr. Prenderbury's scholarly figure in the far corner and her heart lightened. "Now, I expect you to see to it that Harriet remains seated," breathed Cordelia. "I do not need to worry about *you* making an exhibition of yourself, Agnes. No one *ever* asks you to dance." And, with a malicious little laugh, Cordelia floated away.

Agnes took a seat next to the dowagers and looked down at her hands in her lap. She felt tired and miserable. Her pleasure at seeing Mr. Prenderbury had been destroyed by Cordelia's cruelty. She sat scowling horribly as dance followed dance, while the marquess surrendered his post at the door to his butler and joined the dancers, and still Harriet did not come.

And then all at once she was there. Agnes felt a ripple of interest running through the ballroom and looked up.

Harriet was standing at the entrance with the squat bulk of Aunt Rebecca behind her. She looked very sweet and young and tremulous, her large eyes sparkling in the perfect oval of her face. Candlelight shone in the midnight masses of her black hair. She had all the freshness and beauty of youth and spring and first love.

Agnes felt the pain and depression inside her lift and she smiled at Mr. Prenderbury, who gave her a startled look and then hurried to her side.

"My dear Mrs. Hurlingham," he said, "I have been trying to summon up courage to speak to you, but you looked so fierce."

"Not fierce," said Agnes with a surprisingly charming laugh. "Just rather depressed."

He flicked the tails of his coat and sat down beside her. "I called twice to see you, but I was informed you were not at home in such a way as to imply I was no longer welcome."

Agnes took another look at the radiant vision of Harriet to give herself courage and then threw the last remaining vestiges of loyalty to Cordelia away.

"I would like to have seen you," she said, "but I fear Lady Bentley becomes jealous if anyone other than herself appears to be attracting attention. It was she who told the butler not to admit you."

"Monstrous! Can you not leave her household?"

Agnes shook her head. "I have signed a contract for seven years."

"But that is bondage. That is like being treated like a servant in the colonies. Perhaps I could assist you. I have a friend who is a very good lawyer."

"The trouble is that I have nowhere else to go," said Agnes. "I have thought perhaps of offering my services to Miss Harriet and her aunt when they return to the country. I do not eat much, and although they are very poor, I am quite clever with my hands and could perhaps be of help to them. But Lady Bentley would take me to court."

"We will talk further of this," he said gently. "The next dance is a waltz. Pray honor me by partnering me in it."

"Oh, I dare not," said Agnes. "Lady Bentley would be furious."

"She is already so furious with her sister she will not even notice us. Look!"

The Marquess of Arden was holding out his hand to Harriet to lead her in to the waltz. Aunt Rebecca was nodding and smiling. On the other side of the ballroom stood Cordelia with a sort of dreadful stillness about her as she watched her sister.

Harriet was determined to dance. She had never danced the waltz before. Aunt Rebecca, lumbering and hopping like an elephant around the drawing room at Pringle House, had taught her the steps of various reels and country dances. Harriet had only heard of the waltz, that daring and shocking dance where the man actually put his hand on your waist. She had a brief moment's panic as the Marquess of Arden led her onto the floor. But then he put his hand on her waist and her feet seemed to float over the polished floor.

The marquess looked down at her with a disturbed expression in his eyes. He seemed to be looking at several Harriets. There was Harriet, naked under the pump; Harriet, with her hair spilling about her shoulders as she sat at the spinet; Harriet, sooty and dazed, clasped in his embrace above the roaring crowd; and now this Harriet, fresh, beautiful, and achingly vulnerable. He was aware of the malice in Cordelia's eyes, the awakened interest in Bertram's, and all the nodding, gossiping painted faces. He wanted to protect her, to make sure she never suffered a day's harm or hurt again.

He was alarmed at the intensity of his feelings. She was only a woman, after all. If anyone had ever told the marquess that he despised women, he would have been most surprised. But the sad fact was, the only time a woman had not bored him in the past was when she had been flat on her back in his bed. Courted for his title and fortune, toadied to and flattered since the day he was out of short coats, he regarded all of the fair sex with a cynical eye. Romance was for milksops and poets. And yet there had been magic in Harriet's kiss.

"You are looking very beautiful tonight, Miss Harriet," he said.

"Thank you," said Harriet, her eyes very bright with pleasure at the compliment.

"In fact, you are so beautiful I have a great desire to kiss you again."

Harriet stumbled. "You should not speak of that," she said breathlessly. "It was excusable *then* because of the unnatural circumstances, but it is not the manner of a gentleman to remind me of something I would much rather forget."

The marquess felt a stab of pain somewhere in the region of his heart. "Was it so distasteful?" he asked.

"Well, no . . . that is . . . surely all unconventional behavior must be distasteful?"

"An attraction between the sexes is very normal. You will no doubt marry some fine gentleman before the end of the Season and live happily ever afterward."

"Perhaps," said Harriet, and again he felt that odd stab of pain. "No one else seems to marry for love," she said, half to herself, "so there cannot be anything wrong in hoping for a home and security."

"But it is possible to have love *and* security."

"Beggars cannot be choosers. Since I must take care of Aunt Rebecca, I will forget about love and concentrate on security."

"I had not thought to find you mercenary."

"Why not? Everyone else is. 'Tis money that makes the ton go 'round."

He looked at her speculatively, wondering whether she was in fact more like Cordelia than he had thought. Some of what he was thinking must have shown in his eyes, for Harriet once again stumbled and said sharply, "Do not look at me like that, my lord."

"I do not know what you mean," he said. "You must not read things into my expression that do not exist." His voice was sharp. The magic of the waltz faded. Harriet forgot her steps and stumbled miserably through the remainder of the dance.

Her hand was eagerly claimed for the next dance by Bertram Hudson. Once more he saw Harriet as the glorious heroine of his Gothic dreams. He chattered away during the country dance in a bewildering way, since he would start a sentence and continue where he left off some five minutes later when the figure of the dance brought them together again.

Cordelia had never been outshone in the ballroom before. To watch her despised little sister being whirled from partner to partner while the Marquess of Arden leaned against a pillar and watched her with a strange, brooding expression on his hard, handsome face was a bitter experience. She was furious that Harriet should defy her. Back to the country that little minx would go.

The marquess was in fact so absorbed in watching Harriet and in trying to analyze his own confused feelings that he forgot to keep an eye on his young cousin and therefore failed to notice that Bertram was drinking much more than was good for him.

At length the marquess tore his gaze away from Harriet to speak to his friend, Tommy Gresham. When he turned back, there was no sign of her.

Harriet had disappeared into the garden with Bertram.

Flushed with wine and romance, Bertram had decided to propose to her. He asked her whether she would like to step out onto the terrace at the back for a breath of fresh air.

Harriet agreed, since the windows were open and anyone standing on the terrace would still be in full view of the dancers.

The night was very dark and still.

"Would you care to walk down into the garden just a little way, Miss Harriet?" pleaded Bertram. "I have something of importance to say to you."

Harriet looked at him wonderingly. "I will return and fetch Aunt Rebecca," she said. "We must be chaperoned."

"It will only take a minute," he urged.

"Just to the foot of the steps," said Harriet cautiously.

Together they walked down the shallow, mossy steps that led into the small square of garden at the back. The moon came out from behind a cloud and bleached the flowers of a lilac bush silver white.

Harriet turned to face him. "What is it, Mr. Hudson?" she asked.

He gave a sort of groan and gathered her in his arms. Harriet knew he was about to kiss her, and the only reason she let him do so was because she was sure she would experience that same heady sweetness she had felt when the marquess had held her in his arms. But the young lips against her own were soft and hot and suffocating. She jerked her head back and cried out, "Don't, I beg you."

"Yes, don't, Bertram," said a quiet voice above their heads.

The Marquess of Arden was standing at the top of the steps, looking down at them.

"Miss Harriet . . ." began Bertram desperately.

"Please go," whispered Harriet. "You must forgive me, Mr. Hudson. That I should let you behave so!"

"It was just a kiss."

"Please go."

"I am waiting, Bertram," came the marquess's steely voice.

Bertram looked wildly from one to the other. Harriet was standing with her face averted. The marquess's hands were clenched so tightly on the balustrade that his knuckles showed white in the moonlight.

And yet, to Bertram, there was such a strong atmosphere between them it was as if they stood clasped in each other's arms.

He gave an inarticulate gasp and turned and strode from the garden.

Harriet stayed very still. She thought the marquess had left with Bertram. Her cheeks flamed. How could she have behaved so wantonly? The Marquess of Arden would think she was the same as her sister.

A light breeze whispered among the bushes, and from a house nearby came the stumbling chords of a piano as some amateur murdered Vivaldi.

She jumped nervously when she heard a light step on the grass beside her.

"It will not answer, Miss Harriet," came the marquess's cold voice. "You may have your pick of the gentlemen here to gratify your craving for security, but you will not play fast and loose with the affections of my young cousin."

"I was taken by surprise," said Harriet. "He said he had something of importance to say to me."

"Then it was as well I appeared on the scene before the young fool had proposed and you—you had accepted him."

"I have no intention of marrying your cousin," said Harriet wearily.

"Then why did you let him kiss you?"

''I do not know. *You* kissed me yourself.''

''That was different.''

''In what way?''

''Dammit, in this way,'' he said savagely, jerking her into his arms.

Outrage, fear that he took her for a lady of easy virtue, should have caused her to push him away, but that magic came flooding back immediately and she seemed to be turning and turning in the circle of his arms, turning in a spinning world of pain and pleasure, aching longings and unfulfilled desires. They stayed locked together while the wind sighed through the leaves and the faint noises of dancing feet and laughter came from the ballroom. His kiss grew deeper and more intense, and his strong fingers covered one of Harriet's small breasts.

She wrenched herself out of his arms, her eyes wild with fright. She turned and ran up the steps as if all the demons in hell were after her.

''Damn,'' said the Marquess of Arden softly. ''Damn, damn, damn.''

Harriet was quickly surrounded by a laughing group of young men, demanding to know where she had been and clamoring for the next dance.

Harriet dizzily accepted the invitation of the nearest gentleman and allowed herself to be led into a set that was forming for a Scotch reel.

She felt ashamed and dirty. This was what came from having a trollop of a sister, she thought fiercely. No words of love, only savage kisses and that intimate hand on her breast.

It is my own fault, she eventually thought gloomily. It is of no use to blame Cordelia. If I had not behaved like a trollop myself by letting his cousin kiss me, then he would not have been led to believe that I would favor his advances. Her eyes were bright with unshed tears as her partner led her in to supper.

Aunt Rebecca was well content. Harriet had never been in such looks before. Why, her eyes were sparkling like diamonds! They would need to leave for the country as soon as possible. Cordelia would never, ever forgive Harriet her success. But at least they would be leaving with all flags flying.

Aunt Rebecca nodded and murmured some vague reply as Agnes and Mr Prenderbury asked her if she would like a little more to eat. Her attention had become riveted on the Marquess of Arden. He had entered the supper room with several of his friends, but his eyes raked over the room until they finally came to rest on where Harriet sat next to a young officer. As if aware of his gaze, Harriet turned her head, saw him, and blushed.

All may not be lost, thought Aunt Rebecca. Now, I wonder. . . .

Cordelia's temper had been steadily mounting all evening. The Marquess of Arden had not asked her to dance even once. It was all Harriet's fault.

She barely managed to control herself until they were all indoors at Hill Street, and then, with a rosy dawn filtering through the curtains, Cordelia let out all her pent-up rage and jealousy.

She flew at Harriet and tore the flowers from her hair and scratched her face. Harriet, too dazed to defend herself, reeled back. Agnes flew to Harriet's aid and got her face well and truly slapped for her pains.

"Slut!" screamed Cordelia, panting. "Jade! How dare you disobey my orders? You have given Arden such a disgust of this family that he will not come nigh.

Well, you can leave, and take Auntie Frumpie with you.''

Aunt Rebecca burst into tears. Harriet drew back her fist and punched Cordelia in the eye. Cordelia screamed so loudly, her servants came running.

''I order you to take them away,'' screamed Cordelia, encompassing Aunt Rebecca, Harriet, and Agnes with a sweep of her hand. ''Get them out of my sight. You, Findlater, book two places on the coach for Lower Maxton and get these people out of my house. As for you, Agnes, you typical old ape-leader, cringing and fawning over that fool Prenderbury. Be mindful of your duties in future. You will keep to your room until I decide what to do with you.''

The servants stood, irresolute.

Cordelia picked up a vase and hurled it at her butler's head. He dodged it, and it struck the door and burst into a hundred fragments of red and gold and blue china.

''Control yourself,'' said Harriet coldly. ''Do not worry. We are going. I never want to see you again, Cordelia. You *disgust* me.''

Crying with rage, Cordelia seized the poker. With one horrified look at her sister, Harriet put an arm around Aunt Rebecca's shaking shoulders and hustled her from the room.

To Harriet's relief, Aunt Rebecca did not indulge in hysterics once they were in their private sitting room. She dried her eyes and looked at Harriet. ''Do not worry, my dear,'' she said firmly. ''Everything will be all right. We will sit by the fire while you tell me all about the ball.''

''I think I would really rather go to bed, Aunt,'' said Harriet, the scratch Cordelia had inflicted on her showing up dramatically against the white of her face.

''No, please indulge me, my dear. You see, I would

sleep better and feel easier in my conscience if I knew you had enjoyed your one ball. I will ring for some wine to fortify my poor nerves.''

Harriet gave her a watery smile. ''I do not think the servants will answer your call.''

''Nonsense. They still consider you a heroine. Cordelia will be taking her spite out on her poor lady's maid, and the other servants will still be too shocked at the rumpus to go to sleep.'' Aunt Rebecca rang the bell.

A footman answered promptly, his eyes sparkling with curiosity. He politely told Aunt Rebecca that he would fetch a bottle of the best burgundy and then retreated gleefully to tell Findlater that the ladies were set on getting drunk and he didn't blame 'em neither.

Fortified with glasses of wine, Aunt Rebecca and Harriet sat on either side of the fire. At first Harriet talked about how wonderful it was that she had known how to dance and how good Aunt Rebecca's tuition had proved to be.

And then, as fatigue and wine combined with the reaction to Cordelia's dreadful scene loosened her tongue, she falteringly told of the scene in the garden. ''And it was so very dreadful, Aunt,'' she ended. ''Lord Arden put his hand *here*,'' and her own little hand wavered over her left bosom.

''How very shocking!'' said Aunt Rebecca. ''But gentlemen, I have heard, will do the strangest and boldest things when their passions are aroused.''

''I do not think his passions were aroused,'' said Harriet wearily. ''I think he had decided I was like Cordelia—his for the taking. It is a wonder he did not offer me carte blanche.''

''You are tired,'' said Aunt Rebecca. ''Go to sleep, my child. At least we will both be happy to return to our life of hardship at Pringle House. There, at least, we are not subject to Cordelia's whims.''

Aunt Rebecca insisted on sitting beside the bed until Harriet fell asleep.

She lumbered to her feet and softly closed the shutters against the rising sun and drew the curtains. Then she went to her room and changed out of her black silk into an old wool walking dress and covered it up with her usual assortment of scarves and shawls.

The streets were almost deserted. As she reached the corner of Piccadilly, a crossing sweeper gave her a toothless grin and doffed his cap, but Aunt Rebecca had no money with which to pay him, and, raising her skirts, she picked her way across to the Green Park side through the mud.

She hesitated at St. James's Street and then walked boldly down it. Ladies were not supposed to be even *seen* on St. James's Street, but Aunt Rebecca was confident that no one would pay any attention to an old lady like her. She turned left at Pall Mall and looked up at the clock on the Tudor tower of St. James's Palace. Half-past six. Along Pall Mall she went, quickening her step, and turned off up into St. James's Square.

She stood at the corner of the square and studied the Marquess of Arden's town house. A lazy footman was yawning on the step, conversing with a milkmaid.

Taking a deep breath, Aunt Rebecca walked forward.

The last of his guests having left, the marquess was just about to climb into bed when his valet entered, followed by a footman, and murmured that a Miss Clifton was waiting below to see him.

''At this hour!'' exclaimed the marquess. ''Very well. Tell Miss Clifton to wait in my study and I will be with her as soon as I have dressed.''

Convinced that Harriet was his caller, the marquess experienced an odd feeling of triumph.

Come to throw herself on his mercy, had she? Cordelia must have behaved like a hell cat. Well, he would see. He admitted he found her attractive—very attractive. Then he frowned. He could not possibly offer to set up a respectable young lady as his mistress. Pity. He sighed, then shrugged himself into his morning coat.

The look of shock on his face when he surveyed Aunt Rebecca almost made that good lady lose what little courage she had been able to muster.

"Miss Clifton," said the marquess, pulling himself together and making his best bow. "Allow me to offer you some refreshment."

"No, no," protested Aunt Rebecca feebly. "Nothing for me. I am too nervous. My nerves were always delicate." She relapsed into a heavy silence.

The marquess pulled a chair forward and sat facing her.

He looked very handsome, elegant, and remote. His hair was as black and glossy as Harriet's and his eyes looked like agates in the morning light.

A log shifted in the fire, the clocks ticked, and outside the watch called the hour in a hoarse voice.

"What is the reason for your visit, Miss Clifton?" prompted the marquess. "All is well with Miss Harriet, I trust?"

Aunt Rebecca slowly shook her head.

"She is unwell? An accident? Speak, for heaven's sake."

"We are to return to the country today," said Aunt Rebecca lugubriously.

"But Miss Harriet is not sick?"

"She is asleep at the moment."

"Does she know of your visit?"

Again Aunt Rebecca shook her head and again a long silence fell between them.

"I would normally be quite happy to entertain you," said the marquess at last, "but I have not been to bed and neither have you. I do not wish to seem abrupt, but I must ask you to state your business."

The marquess waited impatiently while Aunt Rebecca sighed and tugged at a loose thread on one of her shawls.

"I wish to propose marriage," she said suddenly.

Mad as a hatter, thought the marquess compassionately. He longed for his bed.

Aloud, he said politely, "It is well known I am not interested in marriage, and although you seem an estimable lady to me . . ."

Aunt Rebecca giggled like a schoolgirl. "I'faith, my lord, you flatter me. I do not propose marriage for myself, but on behalf of Harriet."

"I was not aware Miss Harriet hoped for a proposal from me," said the marquess coldly, thinking. The minx! Never say she has told her aunt about that kiss and is trying to coerce me into marriage.

"Harriet knows nothing of this," said Aunt Rebecca firmly.

The marquess's features relaxed. "Then what leads you to suppose I should wish to marry Miss Harriet?"

Aunt Rebecca peered at him hopefully from under the eaves of her bonnet, but he did not look in the slightest like a man in love.

"You will naturally wish to marry sometime," she said cautiously. "Most men do."

"I have not felt that urge as yet, nor am I likely to."

"Oh, but you will," pleaded Aunt Rebecca, "and then you may marry someone quite unsuitable. Gentlemen often do. The curate at Lower Maxton, *he* said he would never marry, not having either the money or the inclination. But he did. He married Miss Oglethorpe, quite a coarse sort of girl. Most unsuitable. But it was a very fine spring, and gentlemen do silly things in the spring.''

"You are well versed in the ways of our sex," said the marquess dryly. "I appreciate your concern for your niece, Miss Clifton, but I am afraid I must reject your very flattering proposal."

"I will find *someone*," said Aunt Rebecca, wearily heaving herself to her feet. "Harriet has worked and slaved to look after me. There must be some man who will appreciate her. She should have a home of her own, and children. Thank you for your courtesy and patience, my lord."

He rose to his feet and bowed, then went to hold open the door for her. "May I offer you my carriage, Miss Clifton?"

"It is not far," said Aunt Rebecca. "I would rather walk."

He escorted her to the step and watched her shabby figure trailing off along the side of the square.

And then quite suddenly he thought of Harriet married to someone else, someone who would hold her in his arms, kiss her, take her to bed, and give her children. Perhaps even Bertram? Bertram had been bitter and sulky before he went to bed, announcing his firm intention of calling on Harriet as soon as possible. He would find she was to be banished to the country and would no doubt propose on the spot, and there was really nothing he, the marquess, could do about it, for Bertram's doting mother would certainly let her darling boy wed the girl of his choice.

Hatless, he ran after Aunt Rebecca, catching up with her in Pall Mall.

"Miss Clifton," he said. "You may tell Miss Harriet I will call on her at three o'clock."

"I will do so," said Aunt Rebecca gravely. "But it would be better to arrange to meet her, say, at the Piccadilly gate of Green Park. I fear Lady Bentley would not allow her to see you."

"Very well," he said.

Aunt Rebecca curtsied and walked sedately off.

That dissipated young blood, Mr. Postlethwaite, stood on the steps of Brooks's in St. James's Street and tried to rub some of the night's fatigue from his eyes. "The deuce!" he said to his friend, Jeremy Pomfret. "There's an old gel covered with scarves on t'other side of the road dancing a jig."

"It's the gin," said Mr. Pomfret wisely. "Pay her no heed."

Chapter Five

The marquess was long to wonder why on earth he had picked such a public rendezvous. As he approached the Piccadilly gate of Green Park, he was hailed by Mr. Tommy Gresham and two of his other friends.

"Where to, John?" cried Mr. Gresham, one of the very few who called the marquess by his first name.

"I am taking a walk," said the marquess. "I am going into the park to commune with nature."

"Don't do that," said Mr. Gresham earnestly, "or you'll get like that cousin of yours and end up writing bad poetry. I say, that's a deuced fine ladybird." He fumbled for his eyeglass and then raised it to admire a young miss who was walking sedately along with her maid.

"I had enough of people last night, Tommy," said the marquess. "A little of my own company would do me a power of good."

"We'll walk with you a little and then we'll leave you to the birds and trees," said Mr. Gresham cheerfully.

The marquess saw Harriet on the far side of Piccadilly. "Look, Tommy," he said urgently as they all moved into the park together. "You are *de trop*."

"*De* what?" asked Mr. Gresham vaguely. "What are you doing, Charlie?" Charlie Brentham, one of his friends, had jumped on a park bench.

"Bet I can walk along the top of it without falling over," said Charlie.

"Bet you can't," chorused his friends.

Harriet appeared at the gate of the park, a slim figure in black.

She looked across to where the marquess stood. Charlie teetered along the top of the bench and then fell with a resounding crash. Everyone cheered.

Harriet turned and started to walk quickly away. The marquess cursed under his breath, then turned and ran after her.

Tommy Gresham let out a war whoop, and he and his friends ran after the marquess. Am I like this? thought the marquess wildly. An overgrown schoolboy?

He turned and put a hand on his friend's large chest. "Down, boy," he said. "Good dog. Go home."

"But—" Mr. Gresham began to protest.

"No!" said the marquess firmly.

Harriet scurried along Bolton Street, her head down and her cheeks flaming.

Aunt Rebecca had merely told her in a mysterious way that she was to meet the Marquess of Arden at the Piccadilly gate of Green Park at three. When she saw him with his noisy friends, her one thought was that he meant to make a game of her. No one who wished to communicate anything important or serious turned up with a party of noisy bloods.

"Miss Harriet!"

She swung about and curtsied.

"I am sorry," he said. "I should have arranged to meet you in a less busy place. Oh, blast! Good afternoon, Lady Jenkins. May I present Miss Harriet Clifton. Miss Harriet, Lady— You have met. Yes, Lady Jenkins, it *does* look like rain, and normally I would be happy to stand on this drafty street corner discoursing on the weather for an age, but I have important business to attend to. Your arm, Miss Harriet."

Despite her nervousness, Harriet giggled. "Poor Lady Jenkins, she looked so startled. Are you usually so abrupt?"

"I usually do not have any reason to be rude. I am anxious to— Afternoon, Colonel. Yes, yes. Looks like rain. May I present Miss Harriet Clifton? Miss Clifton, Colonel Merriweather."

"I say," said the colonel, his little eyes twinkling in a groggy face, "ain't you that heroine who rescued the old Duchess Thingummy?"

"Yes, indeed she is," snapped the marquess. "Good day to you, Colonel."

"Why is London so full of such curst people?" he muttered, leading the way into Berkeley Square. "We will go and eat ices in Gunter's, and if anyone approaches our table, I will *bite* them."

"My dress is unsuitable," pleaded Harriet, tugging at her old black silk gown.

He looked down at her with surprised arrogance. "If you are with me, Miss Harriet," he said, "then you *are* suitable, no matter what you are wearing."

The famous Gunter's was founded in 1757 by an Italian pastry cook, Domenico Negri, who later took Gunter into partnership, making and selling all sorts of English, French, and Italian wet and dry sweetmeats, Cedrati and Bergamet chips, and Naples Divolini at the sign of the Pot and Pineapple in Berkeley Square.

Gunter's was also celebrated for its turtle soup, made from turtles killed in Honduras.

Gunter's ices were famous, made from a secret recipe. But deliveries of ice depended on winds and tides. A small notice in the window stated: ''Messrs Gunter respectfully beg to inform the nobility and gentry who honor them with their custom that this day, having received one of their cargoes of ice by the *Platoff* from the Greenland seas, they are able to supply their cream fruit ices at their former prices.''

The marquess secured a table in a dark corner at the back of the confectioner's, ordered ices for them both, and gave instructions they were not to be disturbed.

Harriet had never had an ice before. She gazed in wonder at the strawberry confection placed before her.

''Where did you get that scratch on your face?'' demanded the marquess.

But Harriet was dreamily beginning to eat her strawberry ice. She thought she had never tasted anything quite so delicious in her life.

What a schoolgirl she is, thought the marquess impatiently. I must be mad to even think of proposing to her.

''If you can tear your mind away from that ice you are worshipping,'' he said acidly, ''you might try to show a little curiosity as to why I wished to see you.''

''Why *did* you wish to see me, my lord?'' asked Harriet, raising her eyes to his. Her gaze was caught and held by his amber eyes. Her spoon clattered nervously against her plate, and she laid it down carefully.

The marquess studied her, from her scratched face under her dowdy bonnet, to the drab black of her gown. He thought she looked a fright. He thought someone ought to take her in hand. He suddenly thought that someone really ought to be himself.

"Will you marry me?" he said.

Harriet looked at him in a dazed way. "Why?"

"Why! Why does one usually want to get married?"

"From what I have observed, for the lady's dowry, her title, her connections, her beauty, so I ask you again. . . . Why?"

The only answer he could think of was that he did not want anyone else to have her.

"I don't know," said the normally articulate and urbane marquess. He began to eat his half-melted ice.

Harriet studied him. Her heart felt heavy. To her horror she realized that she would have thrown herself into his arms right in the middle of Gunter's if he had but said he loved her.

In a slightly tearful voice, she said, "Since your feelings on this matter appear to be somewhat vague, I am sure my rejection of your suit will not trouble you overmuch."

"It puzzles me," he said equably. "I gather you are to be banished to the country."

"How did you learn that?"

"From Miss Clifton. Did she not tell you she called on me?"

"No. I assumed you had sent a footman to Hill Street with a message. Oh, dear, now I have it. Aunt Rebecca asked you to marry me."

"Yes."

"How shaming! You must pay no heed, Lord Arden. Aunt Rebecca is a dear. She worries overmuch about me."

"Miss Harriet, do I look like the sort of man who would propose marriage simply because someone's maiden aunt asked me to?"

She looked at his hard, handsome face, his impeccable tailoring, his easy air of elegance and breeding.

"No," she said baldly. "I do not wish to be insulting, but have you slept at all?"

"No."

"Ah, that is the reason. You do not know quite what you are doing or saying."

This was very near the truth. The marquess felt the whole scene had an air of unreality about it. He felt as if he were in a play. The lowering sky above the plane trees of Berkeley Square cast a greenish light into the dim, genteel recesses of Gunter's. The air was still and heavy. The girl with the scratched face before him was probably the dowdiest-looking female he had ever entertained. And here he was, trying to persuade her to marry him. Ridiculous!

"I have no wish to coerce you into marrying me," he said. "Let us forget about the whole thing. I wish you well in your return to the country. How do you travel? By Lady Bentley's traveling carriage?"

"No, my lord. The stage."

"Then allow me to lend you mine."

"You are very kind, but I must refuse."

"Why? Your aunt would be glad of the comfort even if you are not."

Harriet bit her lip. She remembered that this man had been—or perhaps still was—enamored of her sister. She could not bring herself to tell him that she dreaded the scene that would ensue with Cordelia if her sister found out she was to use the Marquess of Arden's traveling carriage. Harriet felt she had used up all her courage in defying Cordelia by dancing at the ball. She simply shook her head.

"Would you like another ice?"

Again Harriet shook her head.

She felt sick and slightly dizzy. At least she could not be in love with the marquess. Love was supposed to be heady and tender and wonderful. It surely did not make one feel as if one had eaten something bad.

She looked so forlorn that something made him try again. "Think on it, Miss Harriet," he urged. "Last night you were prepared to wed for security. I am offering you that security."

"It is very gentlemanly of you," said Harriet, "and it is very flattering to receive a proposal from such as you. There is no need to marry me. I have almost forgotten our intimacy in the garden at the ball. I am persuaded you were foxed."

"If it makes you comfortable to think so, please do," he said coldly.

The color drained from her face, leaving it looking thin and pale.

There was no use prolonging this painful discussion. All he wanted to do was get to bed and forget that Harriet Clifton had ever existed. He could not even bring himself to think of Cordelia. Another man had lusted after her, a man he did not recognize. Harriet, with her large eyes and dowdy clothes, had taken away his taste for full-blown mistresses, and he did not know how she had managed to do so.

He paid for the ices and escorted her outside. A heavy drop of rain struck his cheek.

"You will get wet," he said.

"I have only a little way to go. Thank you, and good-bye, Lord Arden," said Harriet.

And then she was gone.

The Marquess of Arden walked for a long time until it really began to rain in earnest. He realized he was cold, and his wet clothes were stricking to him. He would feel better after a few hours of sleep.

Harriet found her aunt sitting at the window in their private sitting room. Through the open bedroom doors,

Harriet could see that their trunks were packed and ready. She removed her hat and sat down wearily.

"Well, what did Lord Arden say?" asked Aunt Rebecca eagerly.

Harriet sighed. "He proposed marriage to me, just as you had asked him to do, and I . . . I refused."

Aunt Rebecca's whole face seemed to crumple. "Why?" she wailed, beginning to sob. "He is such a fine man, and so rich and handsome. I do not understand you, Harriet. I am persuaded you are not indifferent to him. It would have meant a home for *me*. Oh, dear, dear. What shall I do? I cannot possibly face another winter of cold and loneliness. It is too much to bear."

Aunt Rebecca was not a saint and therefore subject to as much self-pity as any other human being. For the first time in her life, she thought bitterly that Harriet was a very ungrateful little girl.

Before Harriet's return, Aunt Rebecca had been indulging in rosy dreams. Harriet's wedding would be the greatest affair of the Season. She, Aunt Rebecca, would be the envy of every matchmaking mama in town. They would whisper behind their fans that Miss Clifton was a cunning old genius to have secured such a prize for her dowerless niece. Now all of her magic castles were tumbling about her ears, and she cried and cried.

"Don't, oh, please don't," begged Harriet. If Aunt Rebecca had gone into one of her famous bouts of hysterics, Harriet could have borne it; in fact, she felt she could have borne anything other than this desperate weeping.

"I did not realize I had been so selfish," she said, half to herself. She gave her aunt a hug. "Please don't cry, Aunt. Everything will be all right."

*   *   *

The Marquess of Arden pulled his nightshirt on, settled his nightcap on his head, and climbed into bed. He would sleep and awake refreshed to a world that did not contain Harriet Clifton.

A fire had been lit in his bedroom and the curtains tightly closed to shut out the wet afternoon. The sheets smelled of lavender. He stretched out with a sigh of satisfaction, his eyes already beginning to close. The clock on the mantel ticked soporifically.

And then came a scratching at the door, and his valet entered the room.

The marquess eyed him with one malevolent yellow eye. "What is it?" he demanded. "I told you I did not wish to be disturbed."

"It is a Miss Clifton, my lord," said the valet. "She is downstairs. I would have sent her away, but she assured me that you would be furious if I did so. Miss Clifton said she had an urgent matter to discuss with you."

"Damn the old fool to hell," grumbled the marquess. "Oh, well, it will only take a minute. If she were younger I would show her the door."

"But—" began the valet.

"Show her up," snapped the marquess, staring in amazement at the look of disapproval on his valet's face.

He could not be accused of impropriety in seeing an elderly lady in his bedchamber. He climbed out of bed, pulled on a dressing gown, thrust his feet into a pair of red morocco slippers, and sat down by the fire.

"Miss Clifton," announced the valet in a hollow voice.

Harriet walked into the room, a deep blush staining her cheeks as she surveyed the marquess in all the glory of his undress.

"The deuce!" he said. "I thought my man meant your aunt had come back. Sit down. I will not eat you. In fact, I am quite sure I might even be glad to see you, were I not so confoundedly tired. Well, then, out with it. What brings you?"

Harriet wanted to turn and run away. He had risen at her entrance. Now he sat down again and crossed his ankles.

To her horror, she noticed his ankles were *bare,* and, not only that; he was only displaying several inches of *naked* leg under his dressing gown. She closed her eyes and prayed that she would not faint.

"Sit down," he barked.

Harriet opened her eyes and, staring fixedly at the brass fender, sat down opposite him.

"Well, Miss Harriet, I am waiting."

"I—I have decided to marry you," whispered Harriet.

"What? Speak up and stop mumbling, girl."

"*I have deciced to marry you,*" shouted the much-goaded Harriet.

He leaned back in his chair, made a steeple of his fingers, and surveyed her cynically over the top of them. "So Miss Harriet confronts Auntie with the news she is not going to marry the rich Marquess of Arden, and old Auntie forcibly points out all the disadvantages of returning to Pringle House."

Harriet blushed and looked down. And all in that moment, the marquess—illogically, he thought—decided it might be rather fun to be married. She was delicious to kiss. No other woman had made him feel quite the same. It could not be love, since love did not exist. But it was probably the best he was going to find, and it was time he thought of setting up his nursery. Also, he would be doing a very good thing by rescuing her from a life of poverty. It would mean rescuing Aunt Rebecca as well, but his house in town and his mansion in the country were both large enough to lose her in. He felt a warm glow of virtue as he said, "I am sorry if I was unkind. My offer still stands. When would you like to be married?"

"I don't know," said Harriet miserably.

He rubbed his eyes and yawned. "You had better wait downstairs while I get dressed. The least I can do for my new fiancée is to protect her from her sister's wrath."

"Couldn't I just stay here?" said Harriet.

"No, as the lady I plan to marry, you must be all that is respectable. If Cordelia is still determined to throw you out, then I will house you with one of my relatives."

He rang the bell and told the footman to escort Harriet down to the drawing room and to send his valet.

Left alone in the drawing room with a glass of sweet wine and a plate of ratafia biscuits, Harriet looked about her nervously, hardly able to take in that she was soon to be the mistress of this household.

There was a depressing picture of a deer being torn to bits by a pack of hounds over the fireplace. A stuffed fox glared malevolently at her from a glass case. The furniture was dark and severe. It was a very masculine room and obviously very little used.

She felt she should be experiencing joy and elation. She had captured the prize of the London Season. But the prize of the London Season had seemed so matter-of-fact about it all.

If only he had kissed her or held her close.

She felt so very tired, and the only thing that stopped her from falling asleep where she sat was sheer terror over what Cordelia would say. What had ever happened to create this monster that was her sister? Neither their father nor mother had been hard, mercenary, or selfish.

But Cordelia, for as far back as Harriet could remember, had always wanted the best of everything. Perhaps the fault *did* lie with the late Mr. and Mrs. Clifton in that they *had* always let Cordelia have exactly what she wanted.

Harriet remembered receiving a doll for her birthday. It had been a beautiful doll with nut-brown ringlets and wide blue eyes.

Cordelia's eyes, so like the doll's, had fastened on it, and she had said imperiously, "*I* want that!" Mrs. Clifton had smiled weakly and said, "Well, Harriet, perhaps Cordelia should have the doll because she is *much* more interested in pretty things than you."

Would Cordelia look at the marquess in the same way and say, "*I* want that"? And would he go to her side?

For the first time in her life, Harriet found herself out of charity with her aunt. She felt she had been manipulated.

Marriage.

What would marriage to the marquess be like? Would he bully her? Would he continue to have affairs, as many of the ton seemed to do?

When he finally walked into the room, she looked up and saw him as a stranger: a hard-eyed, competent, sophisticated man, worlds outside of her experience. She felt a suffocating sensation of panic.

He ushered her outside and into a closed carriage.

He rested his head wearily against the upholstery and sighed. "I shall be glad when this interview with Cordelia is over."

He then glanced idly out of the window and said, "There goes the Dowager Duchess of Macham. She looks very spry. I suppose she did not even write to thank you."

Harriet shook her head, wondering that he could be so casual about life when her own stomach was churning with nerves.

It was too short a journey to Hill Street for Harriet.

"You had better go to your room," said the marquess after handing Findlater his card. "Please leave your sister to me."

Cordalia had not been told that the marquess had arrived with Harriet, so she was delighted to see him and considered the fact that he had called without his cousin a hopeful sign.

The marquess, not knowing quite how very bad the situation was at the house on Hill Street, had assumed that Aunt Rebecca had spoken to Cordelia about her hopes for Harriet. Therefore he plunged straight in with "I trust this marriage is not distasteful to you, Lady Bentley?"

Cordelia did not hear the "this" and assumed he was asking, "I trust the idea of marriage is not distasteful to you, Lady Bentley?"

"No, not at all, my lord," breathed Cordelia. She felt a heady sensation of triumph. She had won! The incredible had happened. Arden was about to propose. With one dainty foot, she surreptitiously edged a footstool around in front of her so that his lordship would be comfortable when he got down on one knee.

"I am delighted," he said. "I must confess I was nervous of your reaction." He gave Cordelia a charming smile. "You are as charitable as you are beautiful," he added.

"I do not need to be *charitable*," said Cordelia, "about the subject of marriage to such a gentleman as you. *Any* lady would be proud to be your wife."

"Good," he said briskly. "Let us tell Harriet."

"Poor Harriet *insists* on leaving for the country," said Cordelia laughing, "We shall write to her."

He looked at her with a puzzled frown, and then his face cleared. "Of course, all this must be bewildering to you. She is not going to the country *now*." He laughed. "She would hardly want to miss the wedding."

Cordelia rang the bell and told Findlater to fetch Miss Harriet. Then she gave the marquess a dewy smile and held out her arms. He studied her for a moment with some embarrassment and then walked forward and gave her a chaste peck on the cheek.

"Oh, John," said Cordelia impatiently, but the door opened and Harriet walked in.

The marquess went over to her and took her hand. "Do not look so nervous, my love," he said. "We have your sister's blessing."

Cordelia slowly sank down into the nearest chair. The marquess, at that moment, might have felt nothing more for Harriet than proprietorial possession, and Harriet might only have felt confused and weary, but there was an air of *oneness* about them that struck Cordelia with all the impact of an bucket of icy water thrown over her head.

"You are to marry Harriet?" She gasped.

The marquess smiled at her, taking it as a statement and not a question.

Never had Cordelia's brain worked so quickly. To scream and throw Harriet out would mean she, Cordelia, would never see the marquess again. Also, she was determined to get revenge on Harriet for being so wickedly deceitful, for snatching this prize that was rightfully hers from under her nose.

She tripped forward and caught Harriet's hands in both of her own. "You sly puss," she said. "When is the wedding to be?"

"As soon as possible," said the marquess.

"Oh!" Cordelia's blue eyes flicked over Harriet's slim figure. "Why such speed?"

"I see no point in waiting," said the marquess.

Harriet turned to the marquess and said firmly, "You must excuse me, my lord. Aunt Rebecca is waiting for me. We return to the country. I will write to you . . ."

"Stoopid!" teased Cordelia. "You must be wed from here!"

Harriet blinked at her. "But you said . . ."

"I said, I said," mocked Cordelia. "Sisters are always quarreling. But we love each other nonetheless, and it is my *duty* to make sure you have your family at your side. Alas! The expense of a large wedding. I am not in funds at the moment."

The marquess's thin brows drew together. "I will handle all expenses," he said. "Harriet, take me to your aunt. There are certain matters I wish to discuss with her."

Harriet hesitated, looking suspiciously at her sister, but Cordelia gave her a glowing smile and a kiss on the cheek. Tears of gratitude filled Harriet's eyes and she hugged Cordelia. The fact that they were sisters had overcome any petty jealousies, she thought.

The marquess looked on complacently, glad there had not been a scene. He thought Cordelia had never looked more beautiful or more seductive, and Harriet had never looked so plain and tired. But he realized again that all the attraction Cordelia had once held for him had gone forever.

As he followed Harriet up the stairs, he decided that he had better arrange with Aunt Rebecca to pay a dress allowance for Harriet to her. He still did not quite trust Cordelia, and he was sure she would not use any of her own money to furnish his fiancée with a proper wardrobe.

Cordelia sat, biting her thumb and thinking furiously. God, how she *loathed* Harriet. When her parents had been alive, it had always seemed to Cordelia that they favored Harriet. Harriet was the good one, the baby, the clever one.

After some time, she heard the marquess descending the stairs, but he did not call on her and continued on his way out.

She rang the bell and told Findlater to fetch Mrs. Hurlingham.

Agnes came in, looking pale and wan.

"Sit down," snapped Cordelia. "Now hear this. My slut of a sister has got herself pregnant by Arden, God knows how, and he is to marry her."

Agnes summoned up the last of her reserves of courage and faced her mistress.

"There is no way a young lady like Miss Harriet could ever bring herself to be in such a shameful condition outside of marriage," she said firmly. "I know it, and what is more, Lady Bentley, you know it, too."

Agnes waited for the outburst that she was sure would greet these words, but to her surprise, none came.

"You are probably right," said Cordelia mildly. "Let me think."

Agnes waited anxiously.

"Fond of this Prenderbury, are you?"

Agnes blushed. "Mr. Prenderbury is a true gentleman who has favored me with a certain amount of his attention."

"Humph," said Cordelia thoughtfully. She studied Agnes's face while her companion lowered her eyes and fiddled nervously with her fan.

Cordelia leaned forward. "Think on it, Agnes," she said. "How would you consider the opportunity to entertain Mr. Prenderbury here, meeting him not as a penniless spinster but as a lady with a tidy little *dot*?''

''I have no dowry,'' said Agnes, looking at her mistress in surprise.

''But you could have one . . . if you will but perform a small service for me.''

''Which is?''

''Contrive to poison Harriet's mind against Arden. I have a list of his previous mistresses and can tell you all about them. You will use this information as ammunition. Pity her, in a delicate sort of way, hinting at all sorts of dark secrets in Arden's past until she asks you outright what you mean. Then you will drop the poison in her ear, drip by drip. She will believe *you*.''

''Monstrous!''

''If you do not do this trifling service, which would result in your freedom from the contract, not to mention a dowry and possible marriage to Prenderbury, I will see to it that you lead the life of a drudge. Jobs for servants are hard to come by. None in this house would dare to raise a finger to help you.''

Agnes shrank back in her chair.

Cordelia surveyed her with satisfaction. ''You'll do it, won't you?'' she said softly. ''I know you will.''

Agnes stared at her like a rabbit hypnotized by a snake.

''Lean forward, my dear companion,'' murmured Cordelia, ''and let me instruct you how to strike fear into the virgin soul of Harriet Clifton.''

Chapter Six

Cordelia had never been so popular.

The news of Harriet Clifton's engagement burst upon the ton like a thunderbolt. At first, they were inclined to be maliciously delighted that heroine Harriet had snatched the prize from her sister, but when they quickly realized that Cordelia was on good terms with Harriet and seemed delighted with the forthcoming marriage, they turned against Harriet, calling her an upstart, scheming minx who had entrapped London's most eligible bachelor.

Gossip that Harriet had cheated her sister began to ripple. No one quite knew who had started this gossip, for Cordelia had set rumors about so cleverly that none of it was ever traced back to her.

Harriet was indifferent to shame or blame. Despite her protests, Aunt Rebecca had accepted the marquess's generous allowance and had become positively rejuvenated with all the excitement of taking Harriet from mantua-maker to milliner. And Cordelia, who had planned to shine in contrast to the countrified Harriet, gritted her teeth as a new, modish little sister began to appear.

Aunt Rebecca was quite won over by this new, affectionate Cordelia, but although Harriet was inclined to think—or wishfully think—that Cordelia had changed her ways, there was something about the atmosphere of the house on Hill Street that set her teeth on edge.

Nonetheless, despite the fact that neither she nor Cordelia was honored with vouchers to Almack's Assembly Rooms, that holy of social holies, she was invited to a great number of balls and parties, and she was beginning to enjoy her status as an engaged lady . . . the curiosity of the ton overcoming their dislike of her.

The marquess was present at most of the functions she attended, always polite and attentive. He never saw her alone and showed no signs of passionately seizing her in his arms again.

Although he seemed somewhat remote, Harriet began to hope that the state of marriage might be more comfortable than she had anticipated. Married men seemed to spend most of their time in their clubs or in the House of Lords or on the hunting field. She was glad to be free from all those upsetting feelings that had made her feel so dizzy when the marquess kissed her.

For the marquess's part, he was enjoying the unaccustomed novelty of charitably seeing a young lady well fed and well clothed. In marrying Harriet, he was convinced he was doing a very magnanimous thing.

And so this engaged couple who had so nearly been on the brink of love, failed to see each other as individuals, and each was quite content with the chaste courtship.

The weather had been unusually cold and not at all conducive to romance. Several of London's finest succumbed to the influenza that was raging through the streets, but fear of death did not prevent the ladies from going out in all weathers in nothing but the scantiest of muslin gowns.

There were white frosts at night, and in the red dawns, when society yawned its way to bed, the sooty birds puffed out their feathers and huddled on the branches of the park trees.

It is a well-known fact that no one is truly bad, and so it was that even such a one as Cordelia, Lady Bentley, was subject to pangs of conscience. Although her affectionate manner to Harriet was an act, it was very pleasant to have a sister to gossip to and to go shopping with.

As the marquess continued to be formal and chilly toward Harriet, as Cordelia herself began to attract the attention of the very rich and very old Archie, Lord Struthers, the more Cordelia held back from instructing the shivering Agnes to go ahead and poison Harriet's mind.

And then all at once the weather turned warm and balmy. The normally poisonous London air was now full of the scent of flowers and leaves. Blackbirds sang on the rooftops, and sparrows squabbled and splashed in the puddles between the cobbles. In the twilight, the light at the end of the streets was smoky blue.

Harriet and Cordelia were to attend a rout at a Mrs. Harper's. Mrs. Harper, a rich widow from Boston, had broken with tradition by serving refreshments at her routs. Furthermore, her mansion on Chesterfield Street boasted a double staircase, so one did not have to spend most of the evening fighting one's way up or down.

Harriet was wearing a very smart gown of green and gold striped gauze. Her long black hair was elaborately dressed in one of the latest Roman styles. The dress was wicked in its simplicity and seductive in its effect. The low neckline made the most of her small bosom, and the skirt was cut daringly short to show a glimpse of ankle.

All her old jealousy came rushing back when Cordelia saw that gown. She felt her own creation of pink sprigged muslin was too fussy and sugary by contrast. But it was not the gown that hardened Cordelia's heart. It was the look in the marquess's eyes on seeing Harriet when he called to escort her to the rout. Cordelia at once saw the admiration in his eyes and, what was worse, the tenderness.

The streets outside were thronged with carriages bobbing through the dark, the wavering light of the parish lamps occasionally striking fire from the heavily bejeweled occupants inside.

The air was sweet and warm. The marquess was wearing a corbeau-colored coat and knee breeches. There was a heavy sapphire ring on his finger, and a fine sapphire blazed among the snowy folds of his cravat. He carried his bicorne under his arm. Beside him, in marked contrast to his elegance, sat Lord Struthers, a Scottish peer, the blue of his coat stained with snuff and reeking of brandy and damp dog. Unlike many of the Scottish aristocracy, he had made no attempt to anglicize his vowels, so his conversation seemed to be nothing more than a series of yaps and barks. His corsets creaked abominably, and one pudgy hand in its doeskin glove groped in the darkness for the comfort of Cordelia's knee.

Aunt Rebecca and Agnes had been left behind.

The carriage swayed and lurched over the cobbles, and the marquess's leg brushed against the hem of Harriet's gown. She wondered why that fleeting contact should make her tremble.

Harriet often wondered why the members of the ton did not lose the use of their legs. Chesterfield Street was practically next door, but they had to sit confined in the carriage while the coachman patiently waited his turn.

"We could have walked," said Harriet. "It would only have taken a minute."

"No one walks, my little mouse." Cordelia laughed. "Isn't she sweet?" she mocked, flashing her large blue eyes at the marquess. "So unsullied and countrified!"

Harriet stiffened as she recognized the old familiar venom creeping back into Cordelia's voice, but the marquess said equably, "That is her greatest charm."

He was all at once intensely aware of Harriet, aware of her freshness and youth.

When they finally alighted from the carriage and she took his arm and allowed herself to be led into the house, he glanced down at the calm, beautiful oval of her face under the shining black tresses of her hair and felt a surge of pride and a sudden, fierce feeling of passion.

"We are to be wed in a month's time," he whispered to Harriet as they mounted the stairs.

Her step faltered and she said, "So soon?"

He frowned down at her, and she stammered, "I m-mean, Aunt Rebecca s-said nothing."

"She knows nothing. I have just decided to have an early wedding."

"But all the arrangements," said Harriet. "And who am I to invite? And who is to give me away? There are so many things to think of."

"I have a very good secretary," he said. "He will handle all the arrangements. You should ask Mr. Prenderbury to give you away. He seems to be the only male relative you have. I will ask him for you."

Harriet's eyes looked enormous in the oval of her face. "So-so th-there's nothing really I have to do?"

"No, nothing." He smiled down at her suddenly and her heart gave a lurch.

They had only been at the rout for half an hour when Cordelia appeared beside them, her eyes very bright, declaring that she was bored beyond belief and Lord Struthers had proposed they should all go on to Vauxhall.

"Have you been to Vauxhall?" the marquess asked Harriet.

"No, never."

"Then you should go at least once. I will send my servant ahead to reserve a box."

Vauxhall Gardens on the south bank of the River Thames, was famous for its fireworks and displays. Gone were the old days of the last century, when evening dress was de rigeur and society went on a stately promenade before the fun of the evening began.

The taste of Londoners had progressed without improving, and they were no longer satisfied with the placid joys that had delighted earlier generations.

There was a firework platform erected at the eastern end of the grounds, a firework tower, and a mast sixty feet high from which the "ethereal Saqui" descended the tightrope in a blaze of blue flame and Chinese fire. The ethereal Saqui was in fact, a very solid-looking lady of masculine appearance who was dressed in a Roman helmet surmounted by enormous plumes, a tunic of classic cut, and white linen trousers tied around the ankles and who descended the tightrope on one toe.

A great many of the trees had been cut down, and a large part of the Grand Walk was covered by a colonnade with cast-iron pillars. There were orchestras playing lilting music and singers singing sentimental ballads. There was even a hermit enshrined in one of the groves.

All classes came to Vauxhall, and although society enjoyed the privilege of dining in boxes in the rotunda, the rest mixed freely on the walks, and highly painted, raucous prostitutes hawked their wares and startled the shy Harriet by even producing businsess cards, which they pressed on the marquess and Lord Struthers.

There was a restless, nervous atmosphere. Old Lord Struthers seemed to enjoy it all immensely.

As they approached the boxes down on the Grand Walk, a party of young bloods, led by Mr. Postlethwaite, came whooping along. Harriet was jostled to one side, and when the party rearranged themselves, she found Cordelia was walking on ahead, clinging to the marquess's arm, while she herself was left to follow with Lord Struthers.

"Aye," said Lord Struthers, sighing and gazing after Cordelia, "yon bonny bird has stolen ma hert awa'."

"Indeed?" said Harriet politely, not having the faintest idea what he was talking about.

A frown creased Harriet's smooth brow as they sat around the table in the box and watched the jostling throng below. The marquess and Cordelia seemed comfortably ensconced on one side of the round table, and she and Lord Struthers on the other. Cordelia flirted lightly and expertly with the marquess, claiming Harriet had stolen Lord Struthers away, to which Lord Struthers replied gallantly with something that sounded like "Och, ach, ech, uch."

Lord Struthers consumed a large amount of Vauxhall's famous rack punch very quickly, lolled back in his chair, and began to snore. Cordelia was whispering something in the marquess's ear, and he gave a slow smile.

Color flamed in Harriet's cheeks and she turned her head away.

Perhaps he had only become engaged to her to secure Cordelia as his mistress! But that was ridiculous. If the marquess was bent on marrying someone, then he could always marry Cordelia if he wanted her *that* badly.

There was a grating of chairs. Harriet looked up. The marquess had moved his chair around next to hers and was leaning over her to shake Lord Struthers awake.

"Rouse yourself, Struthers," said the marquess. "I am going to take my fiancée for a promenade and you cannot neglect Lady Bentley."

As she left the box, Harriet turned around to say good-bye to her sister. Cordelia's eyes were as hard and as blue as the marquess's sapphires.

Harriet began to long for the old narrow life of Pringle House, where the discomfort was caused by hard work and poverty rather than people.

"Where are we going?" she asked.

"To watch the fireworks."

"You did not ask me if I *wanted* to watch them." And, to Harriet's horror, her voice sounded pettish to her own ears. Still hurt by his behavior with Cordelia, she added, "You are very kind, my lord. But there was no need to leave the box for my sake. I was under the impression you were enjoying yourself very well where you were."

He looked down at her with a mocking glint in his eye. "I was only being polite to my future sister-in-law," he said. "Do not be at odds with me. Look! Spring is here at last."

But she trudged along beside him like an unwilling child, her lips set in a mutinous line.

They were jostled and pushed along by the throng. A boozy buck turned and leered at Harriet, and the marquess glared at him, then put a protective arm around Harriet's waist.

He felt a tingling sensation go up his arm; he steered Harriet to the side of the walk and then, tightening his grip, pulled her away from the crowds into the quiet darkness of a thick stand of trees.

The chattering, moving, shifting, colorful, motley throng continued on their way along the path toward the fireworks display.

He turned her about to face him and stood, looking down at her.

"What are we doing here?" asked Harriet.

"We are alone," he said huskily. "We are never alone, you know."

"But we are not married yet," pleaded Harriet, "and it is not at all the thing for me to be alone with you without a chaperone."

"Do I frighten you, Harriet?" He put his hand under her chin and tilted her face up to his.

"N-no," she faltered.

He bent his mouth to hers, ignoring her faint murmur of protest.

His lips were firm and cool, and Harriet stayed unresisting in the circle of his arms, accepting the embrace stoically, waiting for it to end.

But his lips grew warmer and more insistent and began to move against hers, and all at once, she felt that dizzying sweetness starting somewhere in the pit of her stomach and spreading throughout her whole body. He pressed her tightly against him until she could not tell where his body began and hers ended.

He finally drew back and she looked up at him and saw a great cloud of golden stars bursting in the night sky far above his head.

"Are they really there?" asked Harriet, dazed. "The stars."

"Yes, they are really there, Harriet. . . . Oh, Harriet, my love."

He bent his mouth to hers again as burst upon burst of fireworks exploded against the sky.

Cordelia, tugging Lord Struthers in her wake, hurried along the walk toward the fireworks display. She happened to glance to the side just as the climax of the display lit up the whole of Vauxhall Gardens, and saw the couple in the middle of the stand of trees, closely entwined, aware only of each other.

"The display is over," snapped Cordelia to Lord Struthers, who was standing, blinking like an owl in the middle of the path. "I am sure Harriet is somewhere near. *Harriet!*"

"Damn," said the marquess softly. "We had better join them."

Laughing shrilly, Cordelia ran forward and put an arm about Harriet's waist. "Naughty puss," she cried. "And you, my lord, are a wicked seducer, as we all know."

On the way back to the box, Cordelia complained of having the headache and said they must go home.

As he left them outside the house on Hill Street, the marquess said, "I must go to the country for a few days to see my parents."

"Your parents?" asked Harriet, surprised.

"The Duke and Duchess of Derwood," said Cordelia with a brittle laugh.

"I am sorry," said Harriet. "I did not think to ask."

"It does not matter," said the marquess. "I would take you to meet them, but I am afraid my father is unwell. I trust he will be better in time for our wedding. If I think he will still be in bad health in a month's time, then I fear we must be married from my home."

Harriet desperately wished that he were not leaving.

She wanted the warmth and closeness of his lovemaking. She sensed the hate coming in waves from Cordelia, and she was afraid.

He kissed her hand, and then he was gone.

To Harriet's relief, Cordelia seemed as affectionate as ever over the tea tray, although she did flirt with old Lord Struthers to an alarming degree.

At last, Lord Struthers took his leave and Harriet went up to join Aunt Rebecca and to tell her about the evening.

"I did not know he was the son of the Duke of Derwood," said Harriet.

"Didn't I tell you?" exclaimed Aunt Rebecca. She settled herself more comfortably among her shawls, two of them new. "Yes, indeed, and Arden inherits the dukedom when his father dies, which will make you, dear Harriet, a duchess."

Cordelia stood for a long moment with her hand on the door of Agnes's room. She remembered the fun and gossip she and Harriet had shared. Then she thought of Harriet becoming the Duchess of Derwood and her pretty face hardened.

She turned the handle and opened the door.

"Wake up, Agnes," she cooed. "Your new duties are about to begin."

Bertram Hudson arrived back in town and went straight to his cousin's, only to learn that the Marquess of Arden had taken off for the country.

He chewed his nails and debated whether to follow him, but on learning he was to return in a few days, Bertram decided to wait.

He had had a harrowing time with his mother. Mrs. Hudson had been in tears. Those scheming Clifton sisters had snatched Bertram's inheritance away from him. After asking patiently to be enlightened, Bertram learned that he was the main beneficiary in the marquess's will. No one had expected Arden to marry, least of all Arden himself.

Despite his sulky ways, Bertram was fond of his tall cousin and had stated hotly that he, Bertram, had a mind above worldly goods and that the marquess could marry whom he pleased and leave his money where he wanted.

But as he sat in the gloomy splendor of the town house in St. James's Square, he could not help thinking that all this, plus the extensive Arden estates and fortune, could have been his.

The fact that the marquess was extremely sound in wind and limb and not likely to pop off for years and years did not cross Bertram's mind. Arden went in for a great deal of sport. His carriage could overturn; he could bring on a heart attack by his visits to Gentleman Jackson's boxing saloon: Anything could happen.

Influenza, typhoid, and cholera stalked the streets of London. Smallpox was rampant. Why, the man could die tomorrow!

And then there was the matter of Harriet Clifton herself. Bertram remembered every shaming moment in the garden.

Miss Harriet would not have rebuffed *him* were he a titled, moneyed lord, thought Bertram cynically. Harriet was no better than her sister and infinitely more cunning. For the marquess had not intended to marry Cordelia, and Harriet had undoubtedly succeeded by strange wiles to enmesh the marquess in her toils. So ran Bertram's Gothic thoughts.

He dashed off a poem—"Oh, Eve! 'Tis *thou* who art the serpent!''—and felt considerably better.

He decided to call on Harriet the following day. He would be resigned, dignified, and slightly pitying. He would flash her a few shrewd looks to show her he was wise to her plots and schemes. All this was very comforting, and Bertram was in an almost cheerful frame of mind when he presented himself at Hill Street.

Harriet was not present, and it seemed a shame that all of his darting, shrewd looks should be wasted on a company that consisted of Lady Jenkins, Mr. Prenderbury, Agnes Hurlingham, and Lord Struthers.

He was planning to cut his visit short when Cordelia drew him aside and begged him to wait until the others had left.

Scenting intrigue and mystery, Bertram brightened and tried to pass the time by talking to Agnes. Agnes was looking very fine in a brand-new gown of India muslin or, rather, would have looked very fine if her brooding gaze had been lit with anything other than flashes of pure misery.

At last, the company left and Agnes was sent to her room.

"It looks as if you might soon lose your companion," said Bertram. "Mrs. Hurlingham and Mr. Prenderbury seem much attached to each other."

"Dreary Agnes is rapidly killing whatever feeling Prenderbury may have for her." Cordelia yawned. "Since she persists in glooming and dooming about the place. But let us not talk of them. I asked you to stay, Mr. Hudson, because I am in sore need of your advice."

Bertram brightened magically. *No one* had ever asked his advice before. Until that moment, he had considered Cordelia a poor sort of creature, his youthful puritan soul damning her as a woman of loose morals. Now, for the first time, he realized how very beautiful and how very feminine she was.

"My problem concerns Harriet and her forthcoming marriage," said Cordelia. "You must help me, Mr. Hudson."

A cynical look marred Mr. Bertram Hudson's young features. Oho! Lady Bentley wanted Arden for herself.

"I am thinking of marrying Lord Struthers," said Cordelia, "and I would like to do so with an easy conscience. Harriet's poverty has made me look like a monster, but the fact is that I have very little money left. You will not repeat this?"

"I swear by—"

"Good. I encouraged Harriet to marry Arden, and I fear I have done a monstrous thing. Harriet is a good and gentle girl, too innocent and countrified in her ways for the likes of Arden. Oh, believe me, your cousin is a gentleman, but he is not of Harriet's world, and he is much too old for her."

"But you and Lord Struthers . . ."

"That is another matter. I respect Lord Struthers. I sacrificed myself once for the family by marrying Lord Bentley. I can do so again. I am a woman of the world, and such arrangements will not soil or ruin me as they would an innocent like Harriet."

She looked at Bertram, her blue eyes growing wider and wider until he felt he was slowly drowning in a warm, tropical sea. He forgot about the poverty at Pringle House, which had been ample evidence that Cordelia had done nothing to help her sister. He eagerly hitched his chair forward. "What can I do?" he asked.

"You must not simply take my word. You must endeavor to get Harriet to confide in you. I think you will find it apparent that she fears Arden and dreads the marriage. Our aunt is very much to blame. Thinking only of herself, Aunt Rebecca pointed out that it was

Harriet's duty to marry well. You may have thought me hard and unfeeling in the past, Mr. Hudson—''

"No, no," cried Bertram, completely won over. This was the stuff of which his Gothic dreams were made. Like many young men of his class and age, he claimed to detest novels. But he devoured as many as he could get, and often the situations and characters in his favorite books were more real to him than anything or anybody in the world around.

"Hark!" Cordelia leaned forward with her hand cupped to her ear. It was one of her favorite "attitudes." Attitudes were very popular among the ladies of the ton. "I hear Harriet returning. Do but stay where you are, Mr. Hudson, and I will send her to you."

A surprised Harriet was told by Cordelia that "that bore of a cousin of Arden's has been plaguing me this half hour. Do be a darling and send him on his way. I *must* rest. Dear Aunt Rebecca, I have a fine Norwich shawl I have been meaning to give you this age."

And so Harriet was neatly left alone to face Mr. Hudson.

She experienced a certain amount of embarrassment on entering the room, worried in case he would remind her of the ball. But he shook hands with her warmly and congratulated her on her marriage—realized his mistake—and, blushing, offered her his felicitations instead. After all, he should have remembered, it was only the man who was ever congratulated.

He was much struck by her pallor. Her beauty appealed to the romantic side of him in a way that Cordelia's more full-blown charms could not.

"I must apologize," he said gently, "for having pressed my unwelcome attentions on you, but the fact was I had had rather too much to drink and your beauty quite overwhelmed me."

"Let us not speak of it, Mr. Hudson," said Harriet awkwardly. "It is all past and forgotten."

"You are most gracious. This engagement—it was very sudden?"

"Yes, very."

"But you must be very much in love to be so precipitate." He saw Harriet stiffen and displeasure and added hurriedly, "That was impertinent, although I did not mean it to be so. I have your welfare very much at heart and my wish is to see you happy. May I act as your escort while Arden is away? It is a lovely day and the sun is shining. We could go for a drive in the park and talk nonsense."

Harriet hesitated. "Come, Miss Harriet," he urged. "We are of an age, I think, and so we can be silly and young together before we have to put on our grown-up society faces for the ton."

His face went through a series of comic contortions, and, despite her worries, Harriet burst out laughing.

She had felt so weary and worried and alone since Agnes had visited her room the night before. Agnes had done her work well. Harriet was dreading her fiancé's return, knowing she would see him for the terrible, lustful satyr of Agnes's description. And Agnes *must* be telling the truth, for the poor woman had choked out the terrible facts as if they were eating her and then had cried her eyes out with remorse. Harriet's first thought had been to write to the marquess canceling the engagement. But there was Aunt Rebecca to consider. Because a man had a dark reputation, it was really no grounds for getting rid of him. Men were allowed such behavior. Women were not.

To expect a man to love with the same spiritual tenderness as a woman was ridiculous. Women fell in love; men had lusts. That was the difference. And so unworldly Harriet tried to resign herself to her fate by dredging up all the dangerous tittle-tattle she had heard from the women in the village when she called at Lower Maxton on one of her rare visits, and combined that with the scurrilous gossip of London society.

Mr. Hudson, despite his carefully adopted slovenliness of dress and his affected brooding manners, seemed kind and helpful. He would hardly press his attentions on her now that she was to wed his cousin.

Harriet glanced out of the window. The sun was glinting on the windows of the houses opposite. The windows of the drawing room were open and a warm, lazy breeze stirred the curtains. Upstairs, Agnes would be weeping. For some reason, the poor woman could not seem to stop crying. Aunt Rebecca would be ready to settle down over the teacups to a long discussion on the state of her nerves.

"Yes, Mr. Hudson," said Harriet quietly. "I would like to go for a drive in the park—very much, indeed."

Mr. Hudson felt very happy. He felt like a knight-errant who had just rescued his lady from the tower. Perched up beside him in his phaeton, Harriet looked beautiful enough to cause a small sensation in the park. She was wearing the very latest thing in hats. It was of the fashionable Egyptian-sand color—Egyptian sand being the stuff sold by stationers to blot letters. It was made of straw and ornamented on the brim by a large cluster of corn poppies. Her poppy-red cambric gown was ornamented around the border with stripes of clear muslin. The sleeves were slashed and fitted tightly over the wrist. She carried a white gauze parasol striped with white silk.

"You are the most modish lady here," said Bertram with satisfaction.

"I am afraid I must be costing Lord Arden a great

deal of money," said Harriet half to herself. She forced a laugh. "It is as well we are to be wed, for if I changed my mind, I could not ever possibly manage to pay him back."

She looked so young and lost as she said this, her large eyes clouded, that Bertram vowed Harriet Clifton should never marry the Marquess of Arden. The fact that one of the pleasant outcomes of breaking off the engagement might mean that Arden would *never* marry and that he, Bertram, would still stand to inherit the Arden wealth would admittedly be a bonus, but Bertram's main motive was gradually changing back to getting Harriet for himself.

"Would you like me to take you to a quiet part of the park and teach you how to drive?" he asked.

"Oh, yes," said Harriet, momentarily forgetting her troubles.

Because Bertram always felt overshadowed by his magnificent cousin, and because Harriet was now very afraid of Arden, they were drawn together. They giggled helplessly over Bertram's attempts to teach Harriet to drive. Harriet felt she was progressing a little along the road to happiness, unaware that she was regressing to the schoolroom and that Mr. Bertram Hudson was falling helplessly in love with her. For the more in love Bertram fell, the more boyish he became.

Cordelia, watching their return from the window, was well pleased. Things were proceeding more quickly than she had hoped. With any luck, she might be able to persuade Bertram to elope with the girl.

And so Bertram's visits were encouraged, and he was allowed more time alone with Harriet than was deemed respectable. Aunt Rebecca, still lost in a rosy dream, saw nothing wrong in Arden's young cousin spending so much time with Harriet. Agnes was too sunk in misery and self-reproach to notice.

A letter came for Harriet from the marquess, saying that he regretted his delay but hoped to be able to return as soon as possible.

Harriet was like a child who has been told that the school has burned down and therefore the summer holidays are to be extended.

She shared all Bertram's enthusiasms, borrowed his Gothic novels, and had even agreed to go to Astley's that very evening with him.

Philip Astley, a sergeant-major in His Majesty's Royal Regiment of Dragoons, was a familiar figure in the West End of London as, mounted on his white horse, he would distribute his own handbills and point with his sword in the direction of his show, which was held on the other side of the river. He was a very enterprising man. When the Dowager Princess of Wales died, he bought up the timber used at her obsequies for a song and roofed in his amphitheater—the theater he had built with the seventy pounds he had got for a diamond ring he had found under Westminster Bridge.

Harriet was thrilled by the display and, unconsciously, clutched Bertram's hand as a pyramid of men on horseback swayed above the audience. She was still, all unaware, holding Bertram's hand when Mr. Tommy Gresham and a party of friends entered the theater. Mr. Gresham bowed to Harriet, raised his quizzing glass, and glared at their joined hands. Then he remarked loudly, "Arden still gone from town?" and walked off as Harriet, blushing, snatched her hand away.

Her enjoyment of the rest of the evening was spoiled. Mr. Gresham had made it all too plain that he thought she was behaving in too familiar a manner with her fiancé's cousin. For the first time, Harriet began to wonder nervously about what the rest of London society was saying.

Bertram noticed she was depressed and silent as he escorted her home and put it down to her worry over her engagement.

Once back at the town house in St. James's Square, he kicked off his boots, sank back in an armchair, and opened up a copy of the latest edition of *The Calendar of Horrors,* a lurid periodical that catered to the current passion for Gothic romances. The setting of a typical Gothic romance of the period was a dank, gloomy castle or abbey, perched on an isolated crag, wreathed in mist, and surrounded by a black, brooding forest. There were dark dungeons, subterranean passages, haunted wings, sepulchral vaults, secret panels and stairways, cobwebs, and bats. The eerie atmosphere, reeking of the charnel house, was designed to make the hackles rise, the flesh creep, and the blood curdle—no easy task in these days of the Regency where people were inured to the gruesome and the macabre by the frequent public hangings and floggings and the sight of criminals' decomposing corpses dangling on gibbets. Most Gothic romances recounted the vicissitudes of a young and guileless innocent, the rightful claimant to riches, who was held in a castle; beset by wicked, grasping relatives or guardians; and terrorized by a host of ghastly creatures, the eldritch denizens of the realms of the supernatural. The eventual discovery of a document, proving the innocent's claim, was followed by a dramatic rescue.

Bertram eagerly began to read the next installment of his favorite serial.

As may be supposed, he was on the spot before the appointed hour, anxiously expecting the appearance of her who was so really and truly dear to him. What to him were the rarest flowers that grew in such happy luxuriance and heedless beauty? Alas, the flower that to his mind was fairer than them all was blighted, and in the wan cheek of her whom he loved, he sighed to see the lily usurping the place of the radiant rose.

Bertram dropped the magazine and sighed gustily, too. Had not the lily usurped the rose in Harriet's cheek as they had left Astley's? How splendid it would be to elope with her, to take her away from all care and harm. They could buy a little cottage in the country with perhaps a few ducks and pigs. Bertram pictured this scene of rustic bliss through half-closed eyes.

But what if Arden really loved the girl? He would soon find consolation, thought Bertram cynically. But he would await his cousin's return and study the couple when they met.

He was sitting in the library, enjoying his dreams, when the door suddenly crashed open and the Marquess of Arden, brandishing a riding crop, strode into the room. With his white face, black hair, and glittering eyes, he looked exactly like the villain in one of Bertram's favorite romances.

Bertram nervously eyed the riding crop and stuffed the magazine behind him.

To his relief, his cousin threw the riding crop into the corner.

"I did not expect your return so soon," said Bertram. "Harriet said—"

"*Harriet?* You are on familiar enough terms with my fiancée as to call her *Harriet?*"

"I mean, *Miss* Harriet told me she had a letter from you saying you would be further delayed."

"Well, as you can see, I was not. Now, pray tell me

what you were doing taking Miss Harriet to Astley's *without* a chaperone? *Holding hands* with Miss Harriet?''

Useless to deny it. The marquess must have come across Tommy Gresham on his way home.

''She seemed unhappy. I was taking care of her until your return,'' said Bertram, trying to look dignified and failing miserably. ''She grabbed my hand because of all the excitement of the show.''

''*She?*''

''Miss Harriet,'' mumbled Bertram.

''What on earth was Aunt Rebecca Clifton about, to let you jaunt about the town with her niece?''

''Miss Clifton did not say anything. Oh, I *knew* you would spoil things.''

''I am going to spoil them more. You are not to see Miss Harriet again unless I am with you. Is that understood?''

''You are treating me like a child!''

''Then behave like a gentleman. Look, Bertram,'' said the marquess in a softer tone, ''I appreciate your keeping Miss Harriet amused, but it has got to stop.''

Bertram stood up. ''If you have quite finished,'' he said, ''I shall retire to my room.'' He stalked to the door, throwing an imaginary cloak over his shoulder and resting his hand on an imaginary sword hilt.

''Oh, Bertram, dear boy,'' said the marquess sweetly.

''Yes?'' said Bertram haughtily.

''You have forgotten your favorite reading matter.'' The marquess held out *The Calendar of Horrors*. Bertram rushed forward, snatched it from him, and ran from the room.

Chapter Seven

Bertram made his way to Hill Street at a disgracefully unfashionable hour—eleven in the morning—and told the startled butler that Lady Bentley must be roused immediately.

Findlater mounted the stairs with maddening slowness, but Bertram had the satisfaction of watching his speedy reappearance. My lady would see him in her bedchamber.

Bertram had never been in any lady's bedchamber other than his mother's. He strolled in, affecting an air of nonchalance.

Cordelia was proposed up against the pillows in no good humor, having had to tear the paper curlers out of her hair and remove her chin strap.

"I hope you have a good reason for waking me up," she said.

Bertram looked uneasily about for somewhere to sit

down, but every chair seemed to be heaped with mounds of clothes.

He advanced and stood at the end of the bed.

"Arden is back."

He had the satisfaction of seeing Cordelia straighten up. "And?" she demanded.

"And he has told me I must never see Harriet again!" exclaimed Bertram, all flashing eyes.

He conveniently forgot that his cousin had merely instructed him not to see Harriet alone.

"But I was under the impression Arden was not to return for several more days."

"Well, he has," said Bertram. "Harriet is an angel. Such a man would crush the bloom of her youth and innocence."

Cordelia blinked and then rallied. "It is a pity," she said, looking at him from under her lashes, "that a strong young man such as you could not persuade her to, er, elope."

"She would never do that. She is all that is honest and upright."

"But were you to persuade her to go on a drive to see—let me see—your mother . . . And if you made good progress on the road north and left me to tell Arden she had cheerfully run away with you, believe me, he would call the whole engagement off himself. He has a great deal of pride."

"I do not have very much money," said Bertram, suddenly feeling very weak and cowardly.

"But I have," said Cordelia, forgetting she had told him she did not have any. "I will supply you with the means to make your escape."

"I don't know," he faltered.

"And I thought you were so brave and noble,"

jeered Cordelia. "Let Harriet marry her marquess. There is no one to save her but you."

Bertram stared at his boots.

"Of course, it would have been a great adventure," said Cordelia dreamily. "I can see it all. The steaming horses; the flight to the north; Harriet, at first shocked, then grateful, flinging herself into your arms."

And yes, all at once, Bertram could see it, too. Had he not just finished reading a romance that had a similar scene? Arden had made him feel like a child. He should be proved wrong.

"I'll do it!" he said. "When?"

Cordelia hesitated. "Tomorrow. Try to get her to agree to go with you tomorrow."

"But today Arden will call and read the riot act. He will forbid her to see me."

"Then see her now," said Cordelia urgently. "Say your mother is ailing and is anxious to meet her. Make Arden appear like a monster. Remind her of your friendship and swear her to secrecy."

"My cousin is not a monster. . . ."

"Of course not. But the end justifies the means. You wish to save her, do you not? She dreads this marriage and is only going ahead with it out of a sense of duty."

Cordelia rose from the bed in one graceful, fluid movement and wound her arms around Bertram's neck.

"Oh, my *hero*!" she breathed.

Bertram's chest swelled. "Never fear," he cried, tossing back his hair. "*I* will save her."

Not yet knowing of the return of her fiancé, Harriet felt nonetheless guilty at entertaining Bertram in the drawing room on her own. Aunt Rebecca was still asleep, and she did not want to rouse Cordelia or Agnes.

Mr. Gresham had made her all too aware of the folly of her behavior. What would the marquess think when he learned she had been seen at Astley's with Bertram?

But Bertram had been kind to her, and she felt an almost maternal affection for him, although she judged him to be about a year older than she.

He launched into the tale of his mother's illness, begging her to go with him.

"Arden has returned," he said.

"In that case," said Harriet cautiously, "it would be as well to ask his permission."

"Which he will not give!" cried Bertram passionately. He sank onto one knee before her. "Oh, Miss Harriet, you do not know my cousin as I do. You only see the softer side of him. He is harsh and arrogant and delights in humiliating me. Surely you have noticed?"

"No," said Harriet honestly. "I think Lord Arden treats you with affection and courtesy."

"When *you* are present, but when we are alone . . . It was always thus. Even with his mistresses. Poor Sally Broadshaw—the opera dancer, you know. She smiled at another man and he *horsewhipped* her."

Bertram sent up a prayer to God to forgive him for maligning his cousin.

Harriet had turned ashen.

"No," she whispered. "I cannot be marrying such a monster."

"If you come with me to my mother's," Bertram urged, "you will have time to think about what you should do. Come, we are always so comfortable together—like brother and sister."

Harriet gave him a shaky smile. They *had* been like brother and sister. The marquess seemed like an ancient lecher compared to this affectionate, naive youth.

"Yes, I would like to get away for a little," said

Harriet. "I shall not even tell Aunt Rebecca. I will merely say I am going to my dressmaker and wish to see her alone."

"Better still," said Bertram buoyantly. "I will call for you at nine in the morning. No one will be awake."

"Does your mother live very far away?"

"No, only a matter of an hour or two's drive."

"Then I will go with you," said Harriet, "and perhaps I will be able to decide on the drive what I must do."

At two in the afternoon, the marquess called and demanded to see his fiancée in private. He did not know he was jealous of Bertram; Harriet did not know he was jealous of Bertram—and so the haughty, angry man who berated her on her lack of dignity, morals, and social sense seemed very much the monster of Bertram's fiction.

"It was all very innocent," said Harriet wearily. "Bertram is so young, so carefree, so much like a brother, I was not aware I was doing anything wrong."

"And yet," grated the marquess, "when I wished to take you aside from the crowd at Vauxhall, ah, *then* you remembered the proprieties and said we should be chaperoned. I thought you were a lady of breeding and good manners, Miss Harriet, despite your unorthodox upbringing. Did not Miss Clifton warn you of the dangers of such behavior?"

"Because Bertram is your relative, she saw nothing amiss," said Harriet.

"Your relationship with my cousin has progressed rapidly in my absence. You call him Bertram, and yet you address me as my lord."

"Perhaps you are regretting your decision to wed me," said Harriet eagerly. "After all, you were rather coerced into it. I will gladly release you from—"

"Release me. *Me!*" The marquess looked at her in amazement. How could she even suggest such a thing, after all his magnaminity and generosity?

Then he noticed her pallor and the shadows under her eyes. "Forgive me," he said gently, "I had forgotten the strain you have been under since you came to London. You are bewildered and distressed and do not quite know what you are saying. Please cancel your social engagements for today and get some rest. We will talk more of this tomorrow."

He bestowed a chaste kiss on her cheek and left.

His pride is so great, thought Harriet miserably, that he will not even listen to me.

But the marquess had received a severe shock. He walked for a long time, thinking about Harriet's behavior and his own.

Then he struck his brow with a dramatic gesture worthy of Bertram and exclaimed out loud, much to the alarm of an elderly couple who were passing at the time, "I have been dishonest!"

He did not want to marry Harriet because it was a fine and generous thing to do. He wanted to marry her because, quite simply, he wanted her. Life without her would be dreary and empty. He had never once said that he loved her. And now he had barked at her and lectured her. Was it not natural she should prefer the company of a youth like Bertram? Did she know how sulky and difficult and cruel Bertram could be when he wasn't getting his own way? Damn Bertram! To be jealous of such a whelp.

She did not have any jewelry. His face brightened. He would buy her a fine necklace, call on her tomorrow, and tell her of his love. She *must* love him. Such a love as his could not go unreciprocated.

Two young belles sighed as they watched his long,

lean, athletic figure stride by. They were very young and very pretty, but the marquess did not even notice their existence.

He felt his behavior toward Harriet Clifton had been that of the veriest coxcomb.

While the Marquess of Arden was walking about the streets of London discovering his love for Harriet, Agnes was entertaining Mr. Prenderbury.

When he was with her, she managed to forget the terrible lies she had told Harriet. They talked of so many things, books and plays and operas.

Cordelia flounced about the drawing room, listening to them in a bored sort of way and, at last, seeing that Mr. Prenderbury was oblivious to her charms, she decided to leave them alone. After all, it was not as if an old maid like Agnes needed a chaperone.

No sooner had she left than Mr. Prenderbury took a clean handkerchief out of the pocket in his tails and spread it on the carpet, rather in the fussy manner of that well-known dramatic actor Romeo Coates, preparing for a Shakespearean death scene, and then got down on one knee.

"Miss Hurlingham," he said, having been assured that her title of Mrs. was merely adopted, "I would be very honored, would vow myself the happiest of men, if you could bring yourself to accept my hand in marriage. Only say the word and my lawyers will free you from your infamous contract to Lady Bentley."

Agnes looked down at him, her heart heavy with guilt. She thought he was too fine, too noble, a man to be allied to such as she. Oh, if only she had stood out against Cordelia!

"I am honored," she said sadly. "Please rise, Mr. Prenderbury. "I cannot accept your offer. There is that which stands between us."

"Tell me," said Mr. Prenderbury eagerly. "There is nothing I would not do for you."

"I cannot," said Agnes. "You must go."

"But you must—"

"*Please*," begged Agnes in an anguished voice. "Please go."

He tried to protest. He reiterated his undying love, but all Agnes would do was to beg him to leave, tears standing out in her eyes.

At last he left. Agnes ran to the window to watch him go.

He stood for a moment in the street below, the picture of dejection and misery.

Upstairs, Cordelia was berating her maid, and her voice polluted the very air.

No, thought Agnes suddenly. I will tell him the truth. This is my only chance of happiness.

She ran downstairs and out into the street, calling wildly after him.

He stopped and turned about, staring in amazement as Agnes, hatless, holding up her skirts, came running along the street.

"I must tell you about it," she said, gasping. "You might never speak to me again, but at least you will know why I rejected your suit."

"Quietly," he said. "Let us go into the gardens of Berkeley Square. We can talk there."

He courteously helped her across the street and into the gardens in the square. The little summerhouse in the center was empty of people.

Agnes and Mr. Prenderbury sat down on a rustic seat.

"Now, my dear Miss Hurlingham," he said. "What is the matter?"

Agnes took a deep breath and blurted out everything

about her lies to Harriet and now Cordelia had threatened to treat her like a slave if she did not obey her wishes.

"Monstrous!" he cried when Agnes had finished, and her heart sank. "To deceive, to ruin the life of her sister, and all out of spite and jealousy!"

"Lady Bentley said furthermore that if I did not obey her"—Agnes gulped—"then I would never see you again."

"This is what I will do," said Mr. Prenderbury. "I am to give Miss Harriet away at the wedding and so I am on calling terms with Arden. So I will call on him and tell him all."

"Oh, *no*."

"Oh, *yes*. It is the only thing to do. As for you, Miss Hurlingham . . ."

Agnes cringed a little away, waiting for his wrath to descend on her head.

"As for you," he went on in a softened tone, "you have been treated shamefully. You will not suffer again. That is what you must do. You must return to Hill Street while I fetch my carriage. Pack all of your things and simply leave. You will come with me to my sister who lives in Bloomsbury, and there you will reside until I arrange for a special license. My sister is much older than I, and a widow. She will be delighted to have your company and to learn that her old stick of a brother is to be wed at last."

Agnes looked at him wonderingly. "You *still* wish to wed me?"

"Of course," said Mr. Prenderbury. "I love you so."

He leaned forward and, with great daring, deposited a chaste kiss on her mouth. But her mouth was warm and sweet, faintly salted from her tears. The touch of her mouth had an odd effect on him. He felt quite dizzy and breathless. So he kissed her again, quite fiercely. And then again.

He pulled her closer into his arms, reflecting that life was full of surprises. He thought he loved her because he admired her brain and her humor. But the throbbing, passionate woman in his arms was a delightful surprise.

"Can you really love me?" whispered Agnes when he at last freed her mouth.

"Of course, you ninny," he said, and Agnes thought she had never heard anything move loverlike in her life.

He resumed kissing her with all the single-mindedness of a scholar who likes to do things thoroughly, only at last becoming aware of his surroundings when he noticed two round-eyed children with a hoop, standing solemnly to watch their performance.

"Come, my love," he said, pulling Agnes to her feet. "We have a great deal to accomplish. "And Arden *must* be told."

But Mr. Prenderbury had to order his little-used traveling carriage to be brought around to Hill Street, after spending valuable time trying to find his underworked coachman. Unknown to him, his coachman had rented his carriage and horses to a merchant and his wife, and it took him some hours to find them.

By the time he arrived at Hill Street, Agnes was near to fainting with nerves, thinking he had changed his mind. Cordelia was gone from the house, and the servants helped her with her luggage, assuming she had been dismissed.

Then there were long explanations to be given to Mr. Prenderbury's sister in Bloomsbury, and when he finally tore himself away from his beloved and presented himself at the marquess's house, it was to be told that my lord was gone from home and not expected back until late.

Mr. Prenderbury decided to leave his interview with the marquess until the morning. Nothing so very dreadful could happen to Harriet before then.

Harriet drove out with Bertram Hudson the next day, relieved that she would be absent when the marquess called.

So relieved was she that she failed to comment on the heavy traveling carriage and the four powerful horses and the luggage strapped onto the back. She had noticed the luggage but had vaguely assumed that Bertram was taking home something to his mother. Nor did she notice that her companion's lips were moving soundlessly. Bertram was rehearsing his great scene, the moment when he would take Harriet into his arms and tell her that her worries were over.

Harriet studied the moving scene outside of the carriage windows. London was so full of people that the main thoroughfares appeared to be a moving multitude or a daily fair.

Off to one side ran the meaner streets, not paved like the main road but with ankle-twisting cobbles and a kennel in the middle. Outside of the West End, London was not beautiful. Apart from the public buildings and the fine houses in Mayfair, the rest of its one hundred sixty thousand houses were not lovely to look upon. They were utilitarian to a degree—long rows of brick-built tenements, with oblong holes for windows. All of the houses were of the same pattern, varied only by the height of the rooms and the number of stories, which were mostly three and rarely exceeded four. There were the front parlor and the back parlor, a wretched narrow passage or hall with a flight of stairs leading to the drawing room. In the basement were the kitchen and scullery.

Harriet let down the glass and the raucous cries of the street vendors filled the carriage.

Chairs were mended in front of the houses, nursery and common chairs with seats of rushes. Repairs cost from one shilling and sixpence to two shillings. Door mats were hawked about, priced from sixpence to four shillings depending on the size.

Turnery was a good street trade, and hawkers were busy selling brooms, brushes, sieves, bowls, and clothes horses.

With a hideous noise, the knife grinder plied his trade, setting and grinding scissors for twopence; penknives, a penny a blade; table knives, two shillings a dozen. Then there was lavender, fish, baskets and bandboxes, hot apples, and cat's and dog's meat at twopence a pound.

The carriage slowed as a watering cart held up traffic, the water dripping from a perforated wooden box at the back.

Harriet grew weary of the moving, shifting scene and picked up a copy of the *Morning Post*. One advertisement caught her eyes.

MATRIMONY—To Noble Ladies or Gentlemen. Any Nobleman, Lady or Gentleman, having a female friend who has been unfortunate, whom they would like to see comfortably settled, and treated with delicacy and kindness, and that might, notwithstanding errors, have an opportunity of moving in superior life by an Union with a Gentleman holding rank in His Majesty's service, who has been long in possession of a regular and handsome establishment, and whose age, manners, and person, are such as will not be objected to, may, by a few lines, post paid, to B. Price, Esq., to be left at the Bar of the Cambridge Coffee House, Newman Street, form a most Desirable Matrimonial union for their friend. If the lady is not naturally vicious, and candor is resorted to, the Gentleman will study by every means in his power to promote domestic felicity.

Harriet laughed. "Would you say I was naturally vicious, Bertram?"

"Not you," said Bertram absentmindedly. He did not want her to speak, for the heroine Harriet in his head did not bear much relation to the real-life Harriet.

The morning wore on, and still they traveled.

Bertram knew that soon he should offer to stop for some refreshment. But he wanted to enjoy his food, so he had to have matters settled between Harriet and himself before then.

In case she enacted a scene, he thought, it would be best to find some private place where they would not be disturbed.

To this end, he finally called to the coachman to stop in the middle of a picturesque village. He told Harriet he was going to scout about on foot because he had heard there was a hostelry, famous for its food, in the vicinity.

"Please let me get down and walk for a little," begged Harriet. They had already stopped twice to change the horses, but each time Bertram had asked her to remain in the carriage.

He agreed reluctantly that there would be no harm in her walking about near the carriage until his return.

Bertram planned to hire someone's house for an hour.

Harriet wandered across the village green. The day was warm and overcast and very still. She felt a long way away from London and experienced a pang of anxiety. She must ask Bertram how long they were going to be on the road. She had thought they would be comfortably back in London by mid-afternoon when her absence would not have created any comment. She had left a note for Aunt Rebecca, saying she had gone out walking and planned to visit the dressmaker before returning to Hill Street.

The coachman, over by the carriage, said something to one of the two grooms, and then they looked across to where Harriet was standing and exchanged sly smiles.

She had not turned over in her mind what she should do about her engagement. She found that thinking about the marquess was too painful. Life with him seemed terrifying, so why did life without him stretch in front of her like a dreary desert?

Meanwhile, Bertram had secured the use of one of the villagers' parlors, exclaiming that his "sister" wished to rest for a little and did not want to go to the common public house.

Having completed the arrangements, he hesitated before returning to Harriet. He was hit by the full force of what he was actually doing. He had lied to his cousin's fiancée and had run off with her.

In his dreams about Harriet, Bertram's future life had always ended at the altar, with only a vague thought of life in a rose-covered cottage afterward. Now he felt weighed down with responsibility. Spoiled by his doting mother ever since he was a baby, and now firmly protected from the evils of the town by the marquess, young Bertram had never known the weight of any responsibility in his life.

The Harriet who was waiting for him so patiently suddenly was no longer the happy-playmate Harriet or romantic-persecuted Harriet but the female he was going to have to marry and support. He thought illogically that it was very selfish of her not to realize all he was sacrificing, forgetting that as far as Harriet was concerned she was merely out on a call.

Like a schoolboy creeping unwillingly to school, he went reluctantly back to where she was waiting and said that the inn was too low and noisy but that a friend would supply them with some refreshment.

"This outing is taking a very long time," said Harriet anxiously. "If I am not back in town by this afternoon, they will think I have run away."

"Not much longer," said Bertram morosely.

The parlor into which Bertram led Harriet surprised her. No one could describe it as being in the first stare of elegance. The furniture was dull and heavy: stiff, high-backed chairs and the type of table the ton only used in their nurseries. The room was dimly lit by one candle, and that was a poor tallow one with a cotton wick. A tall, narrow, and tasteless mantelpiece framed a dull, squat stove of semicircular shape, with a flat front. The tall fire irons leaned against the mantelpiece, and a bowed fender of perforated sheet brass enclosed the hearth. A small hearth rug with a fringe and a bell cord with a plain brass ring completed the furnishing of the room.

A sly slattern of a woman came in and put two pewter mugs of porter on the table.

"May I not present my compliments to your host?" asked Harriet, taking the woman for the servant.

"Not now," said Bertram, looking at the once-imagined love of his life with something approaching dislike.

"Look, Harriet,"he said. "Your worries are over. We are eloping."

Harriet looked at him in horror.

"Aye, well you may stare," said Bertram, beginning to stride up and down. "But there you are. I decided to rescue you, though 'tis sad to be out of London when the Season is at its height."

"Bertram," said Harriet weakly. "My very dear Bertram. I am very flattered, very moved, by your determination to rescue me. But I cannot run away without seeing Lord Arden first and telling him that our engagement is at an end. I wish you had asked me first. We are very dear friends, but I do not think you *really* want to marry me."

Women, thought Bertram bitterly. Well, all they needed was a strong hand.

"You'll do as you're told," he said masterfully. "You are to be my wife, and you will obey me."

"Take me back to London *immediately*," said Harriet firmly. "Don't be so silly, Bertram." She wearily removed her bonnet and shook out her curls.

"*You* call *me* silly." Bertram's face had become suffused with color.

A pin fell from Harriet's hair, and she bent and picked it up. "You must see reason," she said. "Even if Lord Arden is given to horsewhipping mistresses, it does not follow that—"

"Oh, I made that up," jeered Bertram. "God knows all the plotting and planning Cordelia and I have had to do to save you, and yet you do not appreciate it one bit."

"You made it up!" Harriet put her hands to her cheeks. "*You made it up.* You and Cordelia. My dear Bertram, Cordelia is only interested in getting Arden for herself. And Agnes! Agnes who cries so much and looks so guilty! Agnes who suddenly has new clothes and is allowed to entertain Mr. Prenderbury. Cordelia must have told her to tell me all those lies. Oh, God, let me return to London before it is too late.

"Do you not see what has happened, my poor innocent? Cordelia tricked you into this escapade. I am not in need of rescue from Arden, Bertram. I am in need of rescue from Cordelia."

"I will not have you make a fool of me," said Bertram. "Cordelia will already have told Arden you eloped with me, so elope with me you will. Gracious, if he ever found out how I tricked him, goodness knows what he would do to me. You are an ungrateful and unreasonable girl."

Harriet looked at him strangely. "Why did you shoot the hens, Bertram?"

"The—? Oh, the *hens*. They were pecking away and I wanted to try out my new gun."

"And to whom does this house belong?"

"One of the villagers. I rented it for an hour. I had to explain things to you."

"And so you have," said Harriet. "So let us leave."

"You are being silly and stubborn," said Bertram passionately. "You will *marry* me." He looked at her in fury. That such a slip of a girl should stand up to him.

"No, Bertram," said Harriet. She made for the door.

Beside himself with fury, Bertram swung her around and slapped her resoundingly across the face.

"There!" he said triumphantly. "And I will hurt you worse if you do not do as you are told."

Harriet stood for a moment, her head bowed, her hand to her flaming cheek.

Then she drove her fist with all her force into Bertram's stomach. Young ladies of the ton usually did not boast any muscles to speak of, but Harriet had been carrying heavy weights and chopping wood for years.

"I am s-sorry, Bertram," she said, appalled at her own violence.

He staggered toward her, and with a little scream she picked up one of the still-full tankards and banged it down on his head, then ran from the room.

She ran out through the small garden and stood, irresolute, on the road. Unless she hid, and quickly, Bertram would summon his servants.

She turned and ran as hard as she could in the opposite direction, not stopping until she was clear of the village and out in the countryside.

She walked behind a tall hedge and sat down on a hummock of grass, feeling shaken and sick. She had left her bonnet, but her reticule was still attached to her wrist.

She had only a few shillings, not enough to hire a carriage. She would need to wait until Bertram had left and then set out for London on foot. Somehow, she must get back and tell Lord Arden how she had been tricked. But she did not think he would believe her. He had told her not to go out with Bertram, yet she had gone. A large tear rolled down Harriet's cheek. He would never forgive her.

Chapter Eight

The Marquess of Arden had eaten a leisurely break-fast that morning. There was little to interest him in the newspapers.

He looked impatiently at the clock. He was eager to see Harriet again, to tell her he loved her. He had bought her a pretty necklace, and as he put aside the newspaper, he dreamily imagined how it would look against the whiteness of her neck.

He was sure Harriet kept early hours. Better to see her before Cordelia got out of bed.

He dressed with more care than usual, slipped the necklace into his pocket, and walked to Hill Street.

Despite the early hour—it was eleven in the morning—he found to his surprise that Cordelia was awaiting him, dressed in her finest.

"I am delighted to see you, Lady Bentley," he said, kissing the air a few inches above her hand, "but I am anxious to see Miss Harriet."

"Alas, poor Arden." Cordelia sighed. "To be cuck-olded by your own cousin."

He went very still. His face looked older, harder.

"Again, my lady," he said softly. "What did you say?"

"It is terrible," wailed Cordelia, wringing her hands. "Harriet is gone with Bertram. One hopes they will marry. She left a note saying she loved him."

The marquess closed his eyes briefly and then de-manded in a flat voice, "The note, madam. Where is the note?"

"Why, I have not got it! I was so disgusted that she should do such a thing, I threw it on the fire."

"She would not do such a thing," said the marquess. "No matter what it cost her, she would face up to me and tell me she wanted to marry Bertram. Where is Miss Clifton?"

"Asleep, poor old thing," said Cordelia. "The shock was too much for her. I had to administer laudanum and put her back to bed."

"Why did you encourage your sister to go about London unchaperoned in Bertram's company?"

"But I did not! As far as I knew, they only went for drives in the park, which, as you know, is quite *convenable*, provided the carriage is an open one."

"And you knew nothing of this . . . did not know what was in the wind?"

Cordelia looked at him steadily and put her hand on her heart. "By my word," she said, "it came as much of a surprise to me as it did to you."

All at once, he had to get away from her. She, the whole house, the whole situation, disgusted him.

He *hated* Harriet, and he could not wait until he found her to tell her so.

"Where are you going?" asked Cordelia. "Pray stay

with me a little and take some refreshment." She smiled at him seductively.

He looked at her in surprise. "I am going after them."

"Oh, no, you must not," said Cordelia, appalled. What if that fool Harriet repeated the stories she had been told about him? "Only think of the humiliation . . . the blow to your pride."

He looked down at her curiously. "Do you hate your sister?" he asked.

"I?" Cordelia gasped. "Have I not given her a home? Did I not marry old Lord Bentley to alleviate her hardship? Did I not sacrifice myself?"

But the marquess was not Bertram Hudson. "When I called by chance at Pringle House, your sister and aunt were living in abysmal poverty," he said. "One of your gowns, the price of one of your dresses, would have gone a long way to alleviate their hardship. I will never forgive your sister for what she has done, but Bertram is in my charge and must be rescued from his folly."

He turned on his heel and walked from the room. Cordelia stood, biting her lip. Everything was going wrong. Agnes has fled. Cordelia longed to take her to court but knew she would be the laughingstock of the ton if she did so. Why was everyone so *ungrateful*? Hadn't she bought Agnes new gowns and let her entertain that fool Prenderbury as if she were the mistress of the house?

She hoped Arden would be too late to find Bertram before his marriage. Harriet would tell such lies. That girl had always had a sly, lying streak. And after I saved her from death! thought Cordelia. And so she worked on the lies until they had practically become reality. Poor Harriet and Bertram, so young. They would not have a feather to fly with. If she, Cordelia, could not bring Arden up to the mark, then she would just need to sacrifice herself again by marrying Lord Struthers.

When the Marquess of Arden heard Mr. Prenderbury was waiting to see him, he told his butler to send the man away.

Prenderbury had no doubt called to discuss arrangements for the wedding, and the heavy-hearted marquess felt he could not bear to waste valuable time in painful explanations.

He went straight around to the mews to see to the harnessing of his matched bays. After ordering his traveling carriage to be brought around as quickly as possible, he returned to his house.

To his amazement, Mr. Prenderbury was struggling on the steps of the marquess's town house with the butler and one of the first footmen.

"What is the meaning of this?" demanded the marquess.

"I must see you," said Mr. Prenderbury, gasping. "These persons would not let me await your return."

"Come inside for a moment," said the marquess brusquely. "You must speak quickly. I am leaving for the north."

He shouted to his valet to pack a trunk as soon as they were indoors and then led Mr. Prenderbury into the library.

"I thought you had called to discuss arrangements for my wedding, which is why I could not find time to see you," said the marquess. "There will be no wedding."

"I left it too late!" exclaimed Mr. Prenderbury. "Miss Harriet's mind has already been poisoned against you."

"Speak!" said the marquess harshly. Mr. Prenderbury retreated cautiously behind a chair.

"I am to wed Miss Agnes Hurlingham, Lady Bentley's companion—Lady Bentley's *former* companion."

"Good heavens, man, get to the point."

"Lady Bentley had forbidden Agnes to see me. She said that unless Agnes did what she wanted, then not only would she be treated like a slave, but she would never see me again. She told her to poison Miss Harriet's mind against you."

"The deuce! And what did she say that could possibly turn Miss Harriet against me? There are no skeletons in my closet, Prenderbury."

"She told Miss Harriet the names of five of your mistresses."

"So? I am sure even an innocent like Harriet cannot expect a man of my age to have lived like a monk."

"It was what you did to these mistresses." The marquess listened in growing horror as Mr. Prenderbury primly recited a catalogue of beatings and rapes. "Don't you see how wicked and cunning it all was?" cried Mr. Prenderbury. "Miss Harriet would never have believed Lady Bentley, but, alas, she trusted Agnes."

The marquess's butler appeared in the doorway. "Your carriage awaits, my lord."

"Good-bye, Prenderbury," he said. "God willing, you may dance at my wedding yet."

Harriet decided to walk to the next village on the road back to London before finding any refreshment. She hoped her few shillings would be enough. Food was very expensive due to the long war with Napoleon's troops.

The next place she came to was very small, consisting of only a few houses, but it had a very grand posting house with a daunting number of outdoor and indoor servants.

Harriet contented herself with a small meat pie from the bakery and a handful of water from the village pump.

There had been no sign of Bertram, and although she dreaded the weary miles ahead, a long, long walk was preferable to having to endure the sight of him. Harriet now had plenty of leisure time to turn over the perfidy of Cordelia in her mind. She, Harriet, should never have left Pringle House. God was punishing her for sponging off a sister who did not even like her. Harriet tried very hard not to think of the Marquess of Arden because every time she did she experienced a feeling of shame combined with a sinking sensation of loss.

For a time, the walking was pleasant enough. A warm wind had risen and the sun had come out. Her hair was blown about her face, making her look like a gypsy. Her clothes became dusty and the road dried, so the people in passing carriages did not pause to wonder who she was, taking her for some local village girl with her wild hair and her once-modish clothes begrimed with dust.

At a crossroads, the bodies of three felons danced and swayed on a gibbet, and Harriet hurried by, holding her handkerchief to her nose.

But the sight of the bodies reminded her of footpads and the terrors of the night ahead. Once the sun went down, she might become sport for any ruffian finding a solitary woman walking on a lonely road.

She trudged wearily through a flat landscape, ribbons of fields running away of either side. The sun began to sink lower in the sky, and there was a shivering chill in the air. A line of tall poplars beside the road threw long bars of shadow across her path.

Harriet was tired, thirsty, and very much alone. She regretted that she had treated Aunt Rebecca in an off-hand manner. How silly to blame that good-hearted woman of selfishness. Was it not natural that a woman as old as Aunt Rebecca should dread another long, cold winter at Pringle House? Then all at once she thought of the strength of the marquess's arms and the warmth of his lips, and tears made tracks down her dusty cheeks.

She blinked her tears away as she turned at a bend in the road and then shrank into the shelter of the hedgerow. For standing in the middle of the road was Bertram's carriage. She stood where she was, shivering with fear, until it dawned on her that the carriage had neither occupants nor horses.

She walked forward slowly and cautiously.

The carriage was standing at a crossroads. As she approached, she saw the windows had been smashed and one of the doors had been wrenched off its hinges.

She moved around to the front of the carriage. The traces had been cut and were lying in the dust. She looked around wildly, expecting to see Bertram's body in the ditch, but there was no sign of him.

Poor Bertram, thought Harriet with a shudder. He has been set upon by footpads. Pray God he escaped unharmed.

All of her rage and fear about Bertram and his behavior fled, leaving her worried about the carefree boy who had taken her for drives in the park and who had made her laugh.

The Marquess of Arden drove like a man possessed. His coachman sat beside his master on the box with his eyes shut, sure that they would overturn and land in the ditch. The coachman could never understand now his lordship could get his cattle to go at such a breakneck pace. They had changed horses twice, and each time the marquess had stroked the restless animals on the nose and had talked to them. And when he had set out, the horses had reached a fifteen-mile-an-hour pace, which everyone knew could bring on apoplexy. It was an unnatural speed, grumbled the coachman to himself, and resolved to say a few harsh words to one of the young grooms hanging on to the back who had started to sing at the top of his voice, carried away with the excitement of the chase.

Toll keepers felt the lash of the marquess's voice if they were tardy at running out to open their gates.

Some village women crossed themselves in terror as the carriage with its satanic-looking driver sped past, and many said ever afterward that they could smell brimstone.

The coachman never knew quite what happened, but one minute they were racing at breakneck speed along a road toward a crossroads, and the next the marquess had slewed coach, horses, and all right across the road.

He jumped down lightly, holding his whip, and the coachman, who had closed his eyes again in fear, opened them and saw that another carriage had plunged to a halt in front of them, the horses rearing and snorting.

The marquess went up to the other carriage and quieted the horses. Then, ignoring the coachman, he strode around the side and called, "Out! Out of there immediately, Bertram."

There was a long silence, broken only by the sound of water gurgling in the ditch and the clear song of a lark high in the sky above.

"Bertram!" called the marquess again. He went and looked in the window of the coach. There was no sign of Harriet. Only Bertram crouching, white-faced, on the floor.

With a great oath, the marquess swung the butt end of his whip against the carriage windows again and again until all of the glass was splintered. Then he seized the door and wrenched it off its hinges.

"Out!" he said grimly.

"Don't hit me," squeaked Bertram. "I'll tell my mother."

"Where is she, damn you?" raged the marquess.

Bertram sat down on the carriage step and began to cry.

"Stop blubbering," said the marquess, beside himself with fear and rage.

Bertram scrubbed his cuff across his eyes like a schoolboy. "I thought I was doing the r-right thing." He hiccupped. "She seemed to be afraid of you, and Cordelia told me it was my duty to rescue her. It is all Cordelia's fault! It's not *my* fault. I was the soul of courtesy and kindness, and she punched me in the stomach and hit me on the head . . . and then she ran away."

"Where was this? Which way did she run?"

"A village, several miles back . . . That way," said Bertram, pointing down the wrong road. He did not want his cousin to find Harriet until he, Bertram, was well out of reach. He shuddered to think what the marquess would do to him after Harriet told him he had struck her.

"So you simply went off and left her to walk back to London?" said the marquess softly. "Well, a little of your own medicine will do you the power of good."

He called to Bertram's servants. "Get down."

Then he took a knife from his pocket and slashed the traces. "Mount!" he said to the servants. "And ride to London as hard as you can. It may be that I shall be close behind you. If I catch you dallying in the hope of aiding your master, I will make life very unpleasant for you.''

Despite Bertram's loud pleas, threats, and lamentations, his servants quickly mounted and rode off without once looking back.

Bertram thanked his stars he had had the foresight to bring a great deal of money with him. Certainly it had been meant to pay for the costs of an elopement, but now it would do to pay for a comfortable sojourn at a pleasant inn and then for the hire of a chaise to take him back to town.

To his horror, the marquess seized him by the cravat and jerked him upright. His nimble fingers searched in the tails of Bertram's coat and brought out a heavy bag of gold.

"You will not be needing this, coz," he said. "You may call on me later this week and pick it up. Good day to you."

While Bertram stood, dumbfounded, the Marquess of Arden climbed nimbly into his carriage and picked up the reins. Soon he had vanished down the wrong road in a cloud of dust.

Bertram shook his fist at the retreating carriage. "You bully," he raged. "My mother will have something to say on this matter—see if she don't!"

The light was fading fast from the sky. Harriet walked on wearily and slowly. She was hungry and thirsty and tired. She was also very frightened. If poor Bertram could be attacked in broad daylight, then what horrible perils the darkness of night must hold. She had originally planned to sleep for a little behind a hedgerow, but she was too cold, and a thick dew lay glistening on the grass.

Faint yellow candlelight suddenly appeared on her right.

Harriet decided to go to whatever lodging it proved to be and beg shelter for the night. The building was situated on a small side road leading off the main London road.

As Harriet approached, she saw that it was an inn— more of a hedge tavern. She stood for a moment, searching in her reticule. All she had was one half-crown. But that would surely pay for some food and drink. The inn seemed too poor and small to boast any bedchamber other than that of the landlord, but they might allow her to sleep on a settle in the tap.

She pushed open the door and went in, blinking in the candlelight. Four evil faces leered at her. One belonged to the landlord and the other three to his guests.

They are not evil at all, thought Harriet firmly. Their faces are marred by a lifetime of grog and bad feeding.

"I am sorry to disturb you, gentleman," she said. "I am walking to London. There was an accident to my carriage." Harriet did not want to go into long explanations about elopements. "All I desire is something to eat and drink, and perhaps to be allowed to sleep on a chair until daylight."

The landlord studied her from under his beetled brows. Although she was dusty and hatless, her voice was cultured and her gown was expensive.

Harriet waited patiently while the landlord and his guests exchanged glances. She put their tardiness of response down to the slow workings of the yokel mind, not knowing that she had landed in a thieves' den.

Some sort of silent agreement seemed to have been reached among the men, for the landlord lumbered forward, bowing in welcome and wiping his hands on his greasy apron.

"My poor lady," he said, "you must be that tired. Lost yer carridge? Tut! Tut! It warn't footpads?"

"Oh, no," said Harriet.

"Turrible things is footpads," said the landlord. "All oughta be hung."

This seemed to provoke a burst of bewildering merriment from his guests.

"Anyway," said the landlord. "You come along o' me, and you can have a bit o' a wash upstairs, whiles I fetch you a nice bit o' rabbit pie."

"You are most kind," said Harriet, relieved.

She followed him up a dark and dingy wooden stair to a small room under the eaves. The landlord set the candle down on a table. Harriet tried to hide her dismay. The room was filthy and smelled abominable. There was a broken-down bed in one corner covered with a greasy blanket. There were no curtains at the windows, although the panes were so dirty it was unlikely they let any light in or out.

The landlord pointed to a toilet table that held a ewer and a jug.

"There you are, my lady." He grinned. "All the comforts of home."

He went out and shut the door behind him. He listened for a moment, his ear against the panel, and then softly turned the key, locking the door.

"Got her locked up, right and tight," he said cheerfully as he joined his cronies.

One of them cocked his head to one side. "She don't know it, for she ain't started screaming yet. So what we to do with her?"

"Looks like a gentry mort," said the landlord. "Here,

gather 'round the stove and put our heads together and we'll plan what to do.''

Upstairs, Harriet looked at the greasy ewer and the dingy water in dismay. But she should not be so fussy. The landlord was dirty and uncouth, but kind. She had no right to expect more. The room was stuffy and cold, with only a couple of coals and a charred piece of wood smoldering in the fire.

Harriet gave the fire an energetic poking and then stood, looking into the flames, seeing only the Marquess of Arden's face and mourning what she was so sure she had lost. The cheerful crackling of the fire quickly died down. It was then Harriet realized she could hear the men in the tap below talking, their voices rising up through the chimney.

She took a steel comb out of her reticule and began to remove the pins from her hair, and then what the voices were actually saying struck her like a hammer blow.

''. . . so what I say is,'' came the landlord's voice, 'we have a bit o' sport with her to make her tell us whether there's any fambly what would pay a ransom for her. If she turns out to be naught but some sort o' lady's maid, we'll break her in and sell her to some Covent Garden abbess.''

Harriet stood for several moments while the room seemed to turn about her—rather like being kissed by the marquess, she thought dizzily, but not pleasant at all.

Then fear swam over her like a black, roaring wave. She tried the handle of the door. Locked.

''. . . got your piece?'' asked one of the ghostly voices from the fire.

''My gun? Naow. It's under the mattress. *She* won't find it, and if she did, she wouldn't know how to use it.''

Harriet bent down and lifted the mattress. There was a long wicked-looking "birding" gun—a fowling piece with a four-foot barrel. A tin box containing powder and shot was next to it.

Amazed at the steadiness of her own hands, Harriet carefully measured in what she hoped was approximately a drachm and a half of powder. An overloaded gun would be quite capable of dislocating her shoulder. That was followed by approximately an ounce and a quarter of shot. She tested it with the rammer and estimated that shot and charge together came to about eleven fingers. The old gamekeeper at Pringle House used to show her how to clean and load guns when she was a small child, telling her he always liked his fowling piece to have a "full belly."

Jim Marsh, landlord of the Bird in Hand, and his cronies had another round of gin-and-hot before they decided to mount the stairs and see what Harriet was up to.

They could not understand the long silence from the room above and, at last, decided she must have fallen asleep.

The landlord led the way, carrying a candle stuck in a bottle.

He fumbled in his pocket for the key and, before inserting it in the lock, looked over his shoulder to make sure his friends were close behind him. "You all there—Jem, Peter, Harry?" he asked. "Steady, boys, and we'll have some fun."

The door swung open.

Harriet Clifton stood facing them, the fowling piece raised to her shoulder, her eye sighed along the barrel. The candlelight flickered along the length of the barrel.

"Let me pass," said Harriet, "or it will be the worse for you."

The landlord fell back, stepping on Jem's toes. "Go on," jeered Jem. "She don't know how to use it."

"Oh, yes, I do," said Harriet calmly. "Get back and let me pass."

"If you're all cowards, I ain't," said the one called Peter, who was smaller than the rest and had had his view blocked by the others. He pushed past and started to make for Harriet.

Harriet raised the gun and fired. The shot tore into the old plaster of the ceiling and a snowstorm descended on the room, covering it in flakes of white plaster.

The four terrified men turned and ran, down the stairs and out into the night.

Harriet ran after them and slammed the door of the inn behind them. Then she barred the heavy shutters at the window. The inn was well fortified against possible visits by Bow Street Runners. She went back upstairs and reloaded the gun. The window would not open, being sealed with the dirt of ages. Using the butt end of the gun, she smashed the glass and then fired a warning shot out into the night.

Once more, she loaded the gun and carried it downstairs. All she wanted to do was give way to a hearty bout of tears. So she went behind the bar and poured herself a strong measure of brandy and gulped it down.

She hoped they would not set fire to the inn in an attempt to smoke her out. She dearly hoped they would report her to the authorities but was, naturally, very sure they would not.

There was nothing she could do but wait for the dawn and shoot her way to freedom.

It was only after the Marquess of Arden had gone many miles along the wrong road that he began to think Bertram had deliberately sent him in the wrong direction.

He slowed his pace, asking every wayfarer on the road if he had seen a young lady walking alone.

At last, in desperation, he decided to make his way back to the crossroads at all speed to see if he could find news of her on the other road.

At last he reached the crossroads and was about to turn his carriage around into the other road when he saw a chapman with his pack strolling toward him.

"Hulloa, my friend," called the marquess. "Have you seen a young lady walking alone along this road at any time today?"

The chapman touched his forelock. "Reckons I have," he said, and the marquess's heart missed a beat. "Sore exhausted she were."

"Where? Where did you see her?"

"Back there a bit," said the chapman, jerking his thumb in the direction of the inn. " 'Bout a mile along you'll see a liddle turning. Leads to the Bird in Hand. Thieves' den, that is, so as like as not she won't be there. I was having my supper behind the hedge and I sees her go past."

Thanking him and tossing him a coin, the marquess edged his tired team slowly forward. It was a bright moonlit night, but he had no wish to go racing along and perhaps miss Harriet.

He had gone a little way when he heard a shot coming from the left far up ahead.

"Trouble," he murmured. "Hold hard, boys. I will go ahead on foot and see what's about. I have no desire to be surprised by highwaymen."

"Best let that young groom, Billy, go along," grumbled the coachman. "Time he did something 'stead o' singing 'is 'ead off."

"My horses are valuable and I would like you all to prime your pistols and stay here."

He climbed down and began to run lightly along the road.

He began to feel haunted. The moonlight played strange tricks with his eyes. Every tree was Harriet, every bush. Every hummock of grass was an exhausted Harriet collapsed by the road.

As he approached where he roughly judged the sound of the shot to have come from, he saw a low building, a black shape, against the blackness of the trees, to his left, along a lane.

He walked cautiously toward it. If this inn was indeed a haunt of thieves, then before continuing on his search he must make sure Harriet had not been captured by them.

And then a savage blow from behind struck him down.

Moon and stars swung in a giddy circle above his head.

"Well done, Jem," said a hoarse voice. "Let's strip him and then finish him off. That hellcat o' a gentry mort can stay locked up for life for all I care. What pickings. Look at them jools."

Rough hands turned the marquess over. A grimy hand eagerly reached down to seize the sapphire pin from his stock.

But the words had a magic effect on the marquess. In a split second, he was sure the "gentry mort" was Harriet.

Just as the hand reached his throat, he kicked out savagely with both feet and sent one of the men flying. He struggled to his feet. Someone jumped on his back, and, reaching behind him, suddenly feeling as if he had been endowed with the strength of Samson, the marquess heaved the man over his head and sent him sailing off into the bushes.

"There's only one o' him and there's four o' us," squeaked Peter. "At him."

Jim Marsh, the landlord, lumbered forward, swinging his blackjack in his hand.

The marquess watched his approach with contemptuous eyes. "You are too fat to fight," he said.

"We'll see about that," growled the landlord, raising the blackjack, and he rushed in to the attack.

A kidney punch from the marquess doubled him up, and the uppercut that followed it sent him to oblivion.

The marquess swung about and faced Peter, who was creeping up on him, a long knife in his hand. The marquess kicked quickly and savagely. The knife flew from Peter's hand, and there was a loud crack as his arm broke.

He fell whimpering to the ground.

"Where is she?" demanded the marquess, bending over Peter, who was writhing on the ground.

"My lord!" came a call from the road. The sounds of the fight had carried back across the quiet countryside to the ears of the marquess's servants.

"Over here," he called, "and make sure you are armed."

"Now, you," he said, returning to Peter. "Is there a young lady at that inn? Tell me, or I'll break your other arm."

"Don't," whined Peter. "She's there all right."

"Who's with her? How many?"

"She's alone, curse her. She chased us out with Jim's gun."

The marquess's grooms came running up, the coachman having prudently decided to stay and guard the valuable horses.

"Tie them up," said the marquess. "And then go to

the nearest town or village—I think Burming is the nearest—and fetch the local authorities.''

''Oh, lor'.'' said Billy, the groom, surveying the moonlit scene. ''What a mill!''

''See to it,'' said the marquess, striding off toward the inn.

Harriet heard the approaching footsteps and wearily picked up the gun. She was feeling tipsy, having helped herself to more brandy. She had gone into the kitchen at the back to try to find something to eat, but the smell was so sickening that her appetite had fled.

Would this night ever end? So they meant to take her to a Covent Garden abbess? That, Harriet remembered, was the cant name for a female brothel-keeper. Well, she would put the gun in her own mouth and pull the trigger before she allowed them to do that.

''Harriet!'' called a well-loved voice. ''Open the door.''

For one mad moment, Harriet thought she was dreaming. Then she dropped the gun and flew to the door, sobbing as she tore at the bars and bolts.

At last the door swung open and Harriet, dusty and drunk, fell headlong into the Marquess of Arden's arms.

He caught her and swung her up and carried her into the inn.

''Oh, I do love you so.'' Harriet sobbed, her face buried in his waistcoat. ''You must hate me. I didn't know Bertram planned to elope with me. He said he was taking me to see his mother. H-he s-said . . .''

''It's all over,'' said the marquess, cradling her in his arms. ''Shh! Gently now. I want to kiss you and tell you how very much I love you, but I can't do that while you are crying like a watering pot.''

''You *can't* love me.''

''I can . . . very easily. Like this.''

His kiss plunged Harriet into a warm, dark world. She returned passion for passion with innocent enthusiasm until at last he set her on her feet, holding her a little away from him, his breathing ragged.

"My sweeting, my adorable Harriet, you will drive me mad. If you do not want me to frighten you with my ardor, then don't kiss me like that."

"You mean like this?"

"Minx, baggage, and wanton jade. Kiss me again!"

After fifteen dizzy minutes of passion, Harriet suddenly cried, "Your knuckles are bleeding."

"Naturally, my love. I was in a fight."

"I forgot all about those terrible men."

"Those terrible men are tied up outside. My servants will take them to the local authorities or fetch the authorities to them. Now, sit down like a little lady before I forget myself and tell me about your adventures."

He poured himself a brandy and brought a glass of it to Harriet, who was now sitting at a table in front of the stove. "I am sure you have had more than enough already." The marquess grinned. "I have never kissed such a well-seasoned lady before."

"Have you kissed so very many?"

"Never a one like you. I think you had better tell me first of the poisonous lies Agnes Hurlingham told about me."

"So they *were* lies! What made her do such a thing?"

"Cordelia. Always Cordelia. Lady Bentley told poor Agnes, who was already in love with Prenderbury, that if she did not poison your mind against me, she would be locked up, treated like a slave, and she would never see Prenderbury again."

"Poor Agnes!"

"Poor Harriet. Agnes is very well. She has been rescued by the redoubtable Prenderbury and they will be married. Prenderbury told me all about it as I was leaving London. What of that young idiot Bertram?''

''He told me of a mistress that you had whipped. Oh, I must have been out of my mind to believe such a thing! But when you returned to London, the last time I saw you, you were so very angry and—and *cold*.''

He raised her hand to his lips and kissed it. ''I was jealous of Bertram, and it was that jealousy that brought me to my senses.''

''He begged me to go with him to see his mother,'' said Harriet. ''I was so very unhappy and bewildered, I longed to get away for a little. And Bertram—Bertram had been so warm and loving and carefree, very much like I imagined a brother would be. I agreed to go with him. I was so stupid. He had trunks corded up at the back of his coach, but I thought he was taking presents to his mother. We traveled and traveled, miles and miles, until he stopped at a village and said he would investigate the local inn. He returned and said it was too common but that a friend lived nearby. It was a house belonging to one of the villagers, but I did not know that until later.

''When he told me we were eloping and he was saving me from you, I told him I would not do such a thing, that I would return to London and talk to you myself. He became so angry and sulky, and—and . . . he struck me.''

''I'll *kill* him.''

''No. He has been hurt enough. I punched him and then I hit him on the head with a tankard of beer. You must not laugh! I shocked myself. I am not a violent person. And I found his carriage abandoned and damaged. He must have been set upon by maniacs.''

''Only one, my sweeting. It was I. And before you begin to believe again all those horrid stories about me,

Bertram deserved worse. He sent me off on the wrong road. He has been forced to walk back to London."

"After that I ran away and hid in a field until I was sure he had left. I had very little money with me, just a few shillings."

"But why did you not go to the nearest large house and ask for help?"

"I had become suddenly afraid of people. My world was falling about me. No one was what he seemed. Agnes and Bertram, whom I had trusted, had betrayed me. I would not even have come near this inn had I not been so very tired."

"Go on," said the marquess gently. "What happened when you arrived here?"

"There was the landlord and three men. They looked sinister and evil, but people in poor circumstances often do through no fault of their own. He offered me a room, and although the room was disgracefully filthy, I was glad to have shelter.

"Then I heard them talking. They must have been sitting here, next to the stove, for their voices carried up through the chimney. They were wondering whether I would be worth holding for ransom. They said if I turned out to be merely some sort of upper servant, then they would sell me to a Covent Garden abbess after 'breaking me in,' as they put it. They said something about there being a gun under the mattress but that I would never find it, and, if I did, I would not know how to use it.

"But of course I know how to use a fowling piece. And the one I have at Pringle House is equally old-fashioned, having a flintlock instead of one of the new percussion caps. So I loaded it, and when they entered the room—they had locked me in—I fired it, not at them but at the ceiling. They ran away and I chased them out and barred the door. And here I am."

"I hear my servants returning," said the marquess. "I will take you to my carriage and you may rest there until I deal with the authorities. My redoubtable Harriet. You will let *me* take care of you from now on."

He led her out and along the lane past where his servants stood with a small band of the local militia, calling to them that he would return in a moment.

Dizzy with fatigue, Harriet was lifted into the carriage, and warm rugs were tucked about her. His lips pressed briefly against hers, and then he was gone.

Later, she tried to struggle awake when the carriage started to move, but his quiet voice beside her said, "Sleep, Harriet. There is nothing to trouble you now."

She awoke again to feel herself being lifted out. All about was the bustle of a posting house. She was led in to the elegant hall of the hostelry. The marquess was talking and explaining. Then two chambermaids helped her upstairs to a pretty bedroom, undressed her, put her in "one of mistress's nightgowns," and helped her into bed. "I could eat five breakfasts . . . I am so hungry," mumbled Harriet, and then fell asleep once more.

When she awoke, the sun was streaming through the window and the marquess was lying on the bed next to her—but on the top of the bed with all his clothes on and a book in his hand.

He rolled over and kissed her slowly and passionately.

"You see," he said softly, "your reputation is quite ruined, so you will have to marry me. I have decided we will be married here."

"Here?" said Harriet, struggling up against the pillows.

"Yes, here. Far from Cordelia and London scandal. I have already been to see the vicar. We are both to call on him, so I will leave you to dress."

"I am glad to be away from Cordelia," said Harriet. "But poor Aunt Rebecca! Cordelia must be making her life a misery—may even have turned her out in the street!"

"My servants have gone back to London to fetch your aunt, your clothes, my clothes, my servants, a lady's maid for you, my love, and every comfort they can bring back with them. Your new clothes are on that chair."

Harriet looked at the muslin gown and the pile of lacy underthings and blushed.

"The vicar's wife, Mrs. Bradfield, did the shopping." He laughed. "How pretty you are when you blush. Kiss me, Harriet!"

After a few happy moments, he smiled down at her and traced the line of her swollen lips with his thumb. "What are you thinking about?"

"I am thinking that I am so very hungry."

"Poor Harriet. Dress, and you may eat as much as you like."

He swung his legs out of bed and put on his boots.

"What did you tell the landlord here?" said Harriet.

"I told him we were to be married in his village. The tales of your heroism have set the place afire. You can do no wrong. Your respectability is intact. So dress, my love, while I order your breakfast."

He walked to the door. "Oh," he said over his shoulder. "The enterprising Bertram did not walk to London. I am well known at this hostelry, since I often use it when I am journeying to and from London. My estates lie in the north, unlike those of my parents, which are a short distance from town. So Bertram merely strolled in, used my name, and commandeered the best room in the house. He is still here."

The marquess went out and closed the door.

Bertram! Harriet began to dress hurriedly in the muslin gown and pelisse that had been purchased for her. She did not want to see Bertram again.

In another part of the inn, Bertram sat nursing a sore jaw. His large cousin had declared it was just punishment for his having struck Harriet Clifton. All the pangs of conscience Bertram had suffered over his behavior toward Harriet had fled. He felt ill used and misunderstood. He had written to his mother and his servants, and both should be returning together with his mother's carriage.

To console himself, he took out a new copy of *The Calendar of Horrors*, which he had been saving in his coat pocket. So addicted was he to this magazine that Bertram saved up each issue until he could bear the suspense of waiting no longer, rather like a child saving up sugarplums.

He plunged into a new story, and as he read, his eyes grew rounder and rounder. For surely it was about *him*.

There was a young man of dashing and Byronic appearance who was to inherit his wealthy cousin's money. The cousin was a rake and a waster. Everyone agreed the land and estates would be better in the hands of the hero. But then the cousin became enmeshed in the wiles of a seemingly young, fresh, and innocent maid. But the innocent maid had the heart of a Delilah. Nor was she the tender country bloom she appeared, for, underneath, she was a rough sort of woman who could shoot like a gamekeeper and swear like a trooper. Before the marriage, she planned to persuade the cousin to sell his lands and estates and settle in Italy, where she and her evil international companions would shorten his aged existence by introducing him to a round of dissipation and vice. So the hero, desperate to stop the wedding, masqueraded as the vicar. The cousin discovered his beloved was not a virgin and cried with relief when the hero told him he was not really married. The grateful cousin promptly turned over estates and fortune to the hero and went to a monastery.

Bertram read the story over and over again. Hearing the sound of laughter below the window, he crossed the room and looked out.

Harriet and the marquess were strolling back from the vicarage. Harriet looked very happy and very beautiful.

Bertram struck his forehead and then crossed to the mirror and struck it again to see the effect. ''She is a consummate actress,'' he told his reflection.

When Harriet eventually met Bertram, it was to find a penitent young man who begged her forgiveness and then begged his cousin to allow him to stay for the wedding.

''If you must, you must,'' said the marquess, relieved that Bertram was behaving himself. ''I gather your mother is to join us. Well, it will be a family wedding after all. Oh, my love, I had forgotten.'' He drew a flat jewel box out of his pocket. ''I bought this for you.''

Bertram's eyes narrowed as Harriet opened the box and drew out a magnificent necklace of diamonds and sapphires set in antique gold. The sunlight slanting through the window struck the jewels and sent prisms of fiery light dancing about the parlor where they sat. Sparks of light were reflected in Harriet's large eyes, and Bertram thought he was seeing the real Harriet, greedy and evil, peeping through the mask of innocence.

''I am going out for a walk,'' said Bertram, getting to his feet. But Harriet had thrown herself into the marquess's arms and neither of them noticed him leave.

He stalked stiff-legged through the village like a defeated dog. It was some time before he realized a young man was dancing along beside him, trying to thrust a playbill into his hand.

Bertram stopped, holding the playbill gingerly by one corner, for the ink was still wet.

"Why do you choose to perform in such a small place?" he asked the actor.

"Because there's a big market in three days' time. I perform all sorts of roles. I can play the miser, the lover, the villain, the priest . . ."

"Stop!" said Bertram. "Do that again. Play the priest."

"But it is not a good example of my art," cried the actor. "One only has to look pious."

Bertram had had his gold returned to him. He drew out a sovereign and held it up. The gold glinted in the sunlight. "Play a vicar," said Bertram.

The actor was really very good, reflected Bertram. He was a colorless sort of man who only took on features and color when he was acting as someone else.

Bertram took a deep breath. "I have a job for you . . . a job that will earn you more money in one night than you earn in a year."

"Nothing criminal?"

"I want you to assist me in playing a joke on a relative of mine. Nothing criminal."

Chapter Nine

Since the marquess had obtained a special license, they were to be married one day after market day.

Aunt Rebecca had arrived, awash with tears and draped in scarves. She was crying with relief. Cordelia had not thrown her out but had moved her back to the attic.

When the marquess told her of her son's wanton behavior, Bertram's mother, a faded, doting, constantly complaining woman, threw a bout of hysterics to rival anything Aunt Rebecca could produce. Mrs. Hudson became convinced that Harriet had turned the marquess against dear Bertram, and so fueled Bertram's mad ideas by constantly bemoaning the loss of his inheritance and saying Harriet had stolen it away.

"I am taking you far, far away," said the marquess to Harriet. "Aunt Rebecca may go and stay with my parents. They are not strong enough to travel here for the wedding, but I promised them we would be married again from their home. Bertram may go and live with his mother. I no longer care whether he gets fleeced by every card sharp and doxy in London. I want you all to myself. I fear I am giving you a very simple, rustic wedding.''

Harriet was amused at her love's idea of simplicity. The inn was full of his servants, and the kitchen had been taken over by his chef. He had conjured up a lady's maid *and* a wedding dress from London.

Harriet still distrusted Bertram. There was something sly about the boy and he constantly seemed to be acting out a role.

Aunt Rebecca was inclined to be huffy about not being allowed to accompany the couple on their honeymoon, which was to be spent in Naples.

So anxious was Harriet to get away from all of the moaning and complaining that she did not suffer any prewedding nerves at all.

Meanwhile, Bertram and his new actor friend, Jasper St. Clair—real name, Alfred Bennet—worked out their plans. Jasper had studied the vicar from a distance and felt sure he could easily impersonate him. He and the vicar were of a height, and both had brown hair. The vicar wore thick glasses, and it was easy for the actor to find a similar pair.

They planned to attack the vicar when he was alone in the vestry, gag him, tie him up, and put him in a cupboard. There was a capacious one in the vestry. Jasper would then call at the vicarage and tell Mrs. Bradfield her husband had been taken ill. When she arrived at the church, they would tie her up and put her with her husband. All that was left to do then was to tell the vicarage servants that their master and mistress had been invited to join the festivities at the inn and would not be back until after midnight.

It would be left to the fake vicar to tell the marquess after the ceremony that Mrs. Bradfield was ill and that he must return home. Then he would slip out of the door at the back of the church.

That way he would avoid being examined too closely in daylight by the members of the vicar's parish. He knew his disguise would fool even the verger in the dimness of the church. But he doubted very much that anyone seeing him outside would be fooled.

Jasper considered himself the most fortunate of men. He was being paid well for taking part in a joke. Bertram assured him that a generous donation would be given to the church to soothe the vicar.

"Are you sure this cousin of yours is going to enjoy the joke?" asked Jasper.

"Oh, yes," said Bertram cheerfully. "He has a prodigious sense of humor."

He made sure Jasper found a seat at the back of the church during the wedding rehearsal.

Jasper's first sight of this cousin with the prodigious sense of humor was the first thing that made him wonder whether to go through with it. He took one look at the marquess's hard, handsome face and lean, athletic body. He noticed the love in the couple's eyes as they looked at each other.

But the theatrical company was moving on the evening after the wedding. And this Mr. Hudson was paying him a great deal of money.

He quieted his conscience by telling himself over and over again that it was all just a joke. He studied the vicar, Mr. Bradfield, and his lips moved silently as he rehearsed the vicar's high, precise voice.

Next day, everything went according to plan. The vicar and his lady were lying trussed and gagged on the vestry floor.

"Right," said Jasper cheefully to Bertram. "Give me a hand with them and we'll pop them out of sight."

To his horror, Bertram took out a sock weighted with sand and brought it down on the vicar's head and then on his wife's.

"You're mad!" squeaked Jasper. "Why did you do that?"

"We don't want 'em kicking the door and making a rumpus," said Bertram, rather white about the gills. The vicar and his wife looked so frail and helpless that Bertram experienced a spasm of pure terror. He had been acting out a fantasy, and he could not bear to come back to earth.

"Stop squawking or it will be the worse for you," he snapped.

Numbly, Jasper helped him put the unconscious bodies in the cupboard.

"Pay me now," he said.

"No," said Bertram. "You will be paid after the service and not before. You will perform the service correctly—or I will shoot you. Remember, I am the bride man and will be watching your every move."

Strung-up and terrified, Jasper put on the performance of his life. Even Bertram was startled and thought for one awful moment that it was the real vicar.

Ethereal in white muslin and Brussels lace, Harriet felt it was the happiest day of her life. All her worries and humiliations were over.

There was a simple reception at the inn. Bertram was wildly elated, toasting the happy couple and telling several very funny jokes. The marquess smiled at his young cousin indulgently and privately forgave him all. Bertram was young and silly and spoiled, but there was no real vice in him.

The wedding breakfast was finished at about seven in the evening. Harriet's only regret was that the vicar and his wife had chosen not to join them.

The marquess led her up to the bedchamber that had been prepared for them and slowly drew her into his arms. "Now, my lady wife," he said. "I have you all to myself."

The strolling players were moving out of town in the soft twilight, some walking and some riding beside the unwieldy cart that held the company's costumes and scenery.

Jasper was fortunate in that he owned a wiry little pony.

The evening was tranquil and the first star shone down from a violet sky.

Jasper was haunted by the specter of murder. Was there enough air in that cupboard? Had that young fool struck them too hard?

With a sudden cry to the other players that he had left something behind in the village, he swung his pony around and clattered back down the road.

Hoping the church would not be locked, he crept around to the back door and gently turned the handle. To his relief, the door opened. He fumbled in the darkness of the vestry until he found a candle. For a while, he thought the flint on his tinderbox would never spark, but at last he succeeded in lighting the candle.

He unlocked the cupboard door and held the candle high. The vicar and his wife, blinking like owls, glared up at him.

"Oh, merciful God, you are still alive," breathed Jasper. He took out his knife and cut the bonds that held their wrists.

"Forgive me," he whispered, and then turned and ran.

He mounted his pony and set out after the other players. Sovereigns paid to him by Bertram jingled happily in his pocket. He did not fear a chase by the law, for the marquess would not want to see his own cousin in court. But that marquess would certainly give young Bertram a hiding.

And, at that merry thought, Jasper began to sing, and was still singing happily when he caught up with the company.

Harriet was afloat on a sea of love. Naked as the first time the marquess had seen her, she lay wrapped in his arms. He had spent a long time kissing and caressing her, afraid of frightening her.

But passion was making them frantic. "Now, my wife," whispered the marquess, and the broad shield of his chest rose before Harriet's eyes.

"Stop!" screamed a voice from the doorway.

And then the room was full of people, lights, and noise.

Harriet screamed and dragged the blanket over her body as the marquess rolled to one side. She dragged them up to her chin, her enormous, frightened eyes peering over the top.

"What in hell's name . . . ?" roared the marquess. "Bradfield!" he exclaimed, recognizing the vicar. "What on earth are you about, to burst in on me?"

"You are not married!" cried the vicar. "You are in mortal sin."

Aunt Rebecca appeared behind the vicar, and Mrs. Hudson behind her.

"But you married us yourself," said the marquess.

"No, my lord," said the landlord. "Vicar says as

how some actor 'personated him, and young Mr. Hudson hit him and the missus on the head and stuffed them in the vestry cupboard.''

''No!'' screamed Mrs. Hudson. ''I must find my poor boy.''

''*You* will find your poor boy?'' raged the marquess. ''*I*, madam, will find your poor boy, and when I do, I will put him in Bedlam.''

''The question is, my lord,'' said the vicar, turning red. ''Have you, er, um?''

''Have I consummated my nonmarriage? No, dammit, I have not. Clear the room while I dress. I will find that Bertram no matter where he is hiding.''

''He must wait,'' said the vicar firmly. ''You must be married right away. Ah, my dear,'' he added as his wife, looking pale and flustered, appeared in the doorway with his robes, ''you are just in time. Help me on with my robes. Landlord, you must stand in as bride man. Go to his lordship's side of the bed. Miss Clifton, be so good as to give the landlord, Mr. Hoskins, your ring. And the elder Miss Clifton, be so good as to go to your niece's side of the bed.''

Surprisingly calm, Aunt Rebecca did as she was bidden.

Harriet gazed at them all, wide-eyed.

''Are we really going to be married like *this*?'' she asked the marquess.

''It seems we must. Get on with it, Reverend.''

The marquess arranged the blankets comfortably over his naked body and propped himself up on the pillow.

''Dearly beloved,'' began the vicar, ''we are gathered together. . . .''

In a bewildered little voice, Harriet gave her responses.

The vicar and his wife were so embarrassed at having

to officiate at the wedding of this naked couple that they departed as soon as the marquess and Harriet were made man and wife.

"Now," said the marquess when they were alone again, "where was I?"

"What about Bertram?" asked Harriet.

"Damn Bertram. I'll kill him tomorrow. Oh, Harriet, my life . . . my wife . . ."

Cordelia did not learn of Harriet's wedding until two weeks after it took place. It was a discreet little notice, with no mention of fake vicars, erring cousins, or any scandal whatsoever.

She bit her lip. One humiliation after another. Agnes was to be married in two months' time. Society would know very well that she, Cordelia, had not been invited to her sister's wedding.

For a while, she felt miserable and ashamed. If only she had left things alone. She now realized that she had had all the respectability she craved when she and Harriet had been, on the face of it at least, friends. But after a while she hardened her heart and decided nothing was her fault. Hadn't she tried to do her best for Harriet? Bertram Hudson would have made her a very suitable husband.

Cordelia decided to wed Lord Struthers. He was extremely rich, and he would not live very long.

She canceled her engagements for the evening and sent a footman with a note to Lord Struthers inviting him to supper.

She not only plied his lordship with a great deal of wine, but drank a great deal of it herself in order to face what lay ahead.

What took place in the silken sheets in Cordelia's bedchamber is best left to the imagination, but Cordelia was finally able to feel much easier in her conscience. She had *worked* for her money. Lord Bentley had hardly been an Adonis, but this elderly Scots satyr was infinitely worse.

But she had played her part well. She could now get some well-earned sleep and gracefully accept his proposal in the morning.

To her irritation, the bed began to creak and groan as Lord Struthers heaved his bulk out of it. He put on his clothes with remarkable speed for such an old man.

"There is no need to rush off," said Cordelia sleepily. "Where are you going?"

"Back tae ma ain bed," said his lordship, stuffing his shirt into his breeches.

"But this is your bed now, my love," cooed Cordelia, "or will be until we are wed."

He finished dressing, seeming not to hear.

Then he walked toward the bed and threw a heavy bag of gold on the table next to Cordelia's head.

"What's this?" asked Cordelia, struggling up from under the blankets.

"I usually pay ma women," said Lord Struthers with simple pride.

Cordelia could not believe what was happening to her. She tried to laugh.

"But we are to be married!"

"Merrit? Us?" Lord Struthers began to laugh. "Ma dear lassie, we dinna merry the likes o' you."

Cordelia seized the bag of gold and threw it at his head.

With surprising speed, Lord Struthers nipped out of the bedroom door and down the stairs.

Cordelia cried long and lustily before she at last crawled from bed and began to pick up the scattered guineas from the floor.

*   *   *

Harriet and her lord spent a long honeymoon in Naples, returning to London to find it in the grip of one of the coldest winters in memory.

"It is so good to be home." The marquess sighed. Harriet looking around the gloom of St. James's Square, remembered the sunshine of Naples, shuddered.

"Do you think, my love," she ventured, "that I could have one room to decorate? A drawing room, perhaps?"

"What is wrong with this one?" asked the marquess, looking about.

"It is so dark," said Harriet. "And all those paintings of slaughtered animals."

"Perhaps you are right," said the marquess vaguely. "Do what you like with it. Do anything you like so long as you come upstairs with me and celebrate our return home."

"Oh, Arden," said Harriet dreamily. "I cannot believe you still love me."

"Please call me John and break with tradition," he begged. "Let the rest of the ton address one another in bed as if they are in their drawing rooms. I like to hear my name of your lips."

"John."

"That's better. Oh, damn. Here comes Mrs. Hudson. We will not see her."

"But I can hear her crying," said Harriet. "Please. She sounds in great distress."

"Very well."

Mrs. Hudson presented a dismal sight. She was draped from head to foot in black.

"My poor Mrs. Hudson. Why are you in mourning?" cried Harriet. "Is Bertram . . . ?"

"He must be." Mrs. Hudson sobbed into a black-edged handkerchief. "Ever since your wedding, he has been missing. He must be dead. He would never abandon me like this. Oh, Arden, you *must* find him for me. You must!"

"Why should I make any effort to bring that jackanapes back into my life?" asked the marquess. "He is lucky I did not manage to find him, or you would have every reason to be in mourning."

"Oh, hush," said Harriet, her kind heart touched. "I am sure we will do all we can."

But it took all of Harriet's powers of persuasion to convince the marquess to attempt to find Bertram. "I shall come with you," said Harriet. "We shall go back to that village where we were married."

"If we tried before and could not find him, it is unlikely we will be successful after all this time," grumbled the marquess.

At last, he gave Mrs. Hudson his promise to look for Bertram, and she left, still crying.

The marquess rang for his secretary and asked if there had been any letter from Bertram during their absence.

"No, my lord," said the secretary. "I opened and read all the mail as you requested. There have been various complaints from her grace, your mother, wondering when she can get rid of Miss Clifton—I beg your pardon, my lady, I was merely using her grace's very words."

"I wish we had stayed away," grumbled the marquess. "Send a carriage to my parents' home to convey Miss Clifton here, and tell them I shall visit them shortly to arrange a formal wedding ceremony. A plague on all these people!"

It was a week before he and Harriet started their

search for Bertram. The vicar, Mr. Bradfield, and his wife were delighted to see them.

"I cannot think too hardly of that actor even though he impersonated me," said the vicar as his wife served tea. "He appeared most repentant."

"I thought Bertram might have joined that company of players when I rode after them," said the marquess. "But they all swore they had not seen hide nor hair of him or that Jasper fellow."

"I wonder," said the vicar. "Actors are like children. They often make very good liars because for that moment they *believe* the lie and they look at you with all the solemn innocence of children.

"I remember one autumn a group of players came to perform at the harvest festival. I saw them stealing apples from my orchard.

"When I accused them of it, they looked at me with hurt expressions and explained that my trees had a certain rare disease and they were trying to help me by applying a certain *tree medicine* to the bark. Amazing! I almost believed them.

"Now, your cousin was probably not of their company, but it is more than possible this Jasper was. They live on the fringes of the law and are expert at protecting one of their own."

"Have they been here again?" asked the marquess.

"No. But I did hear they were over at Little Champton."

"We shall try there," said the marquess. "Mayhap we might find this Jasper and that will be a start."

As they drove out in the direction of Little Champton, which was some ten miles away, the marquess told Harriet that it would perhaps be better to attend the performance. If they called beforehand, then Jasper would be warned of their presence.

The performance was called *The Feast of Blood* and promised "horrors extraordinary." Ladies were advised to have not only their vinaigrettes handy but also a "strong gentleman" to bear them home when they fainted "from excess of emotion."

The marquess studied the names on the playbill. There was no Jasper St. Clair listed. The main attraction appeared to be that "Drury Lane actor, beloved by the crown'd heads of Europe and Asia, Lord Peregrine Divine."

"How these mountebanks do love to elevate themselves to the peerage," murmured the marquess. "It is a wonder the authorities have not arrested him."

The performance was held in an old barn outside the town. It was amazingly full, and Harriet was surprised to see a number of elegantly dressed ladies and gentlemen in the front benches.

"Lord Peregrine Divine appears to have quite a following," commented the marquess.

To make up for the paucity of the scenery, the play had a narrator. He was a slim young man, too tall and thin to be Jasper St. Clair.

In gloomy tones, he started to speak.

"The solemn tones of an old cathedral clock have announced midnight. . . ." Someone banged a saucepan lid offstage twelve times, and the audience giggled. The narrator glared at them and went on. "The air is thick and heavy—a strange, deathlike stillness pervades all nature. Like the ominous calm that precedes some more than usually terrific outbreak of the elements, they seemed to have paused even in their ordinary fluctuations, to gather a terrific strength for the great effort. A faint peal of thunder now comes from far off. Like a signal gun for the battle of the winds to begin, it appeared to wake them from their lethargy, and one awful, warring hurricane swept over a whole city, producing more devastation in the four or five minutes it lasted than would half a century of ordinary phenomena.''

The narrator then knocked over a kitchen chair to illustrate devastation and made a gloomy exit.

And then, all swinging cloak and flashing eyes, Lord Peregrine Divine strode onto the stage and the audience cheered themselves hoarse, while he glared at them with aristocratic contempt before speaking the ringing lines, ''What ho, Slyvester, my trusted servant. Art in yon tavern? I need thy help, for my love, the Duchess of Pellegrino, lies buried in yon crumbling ruins.''

''Oh, dear,'' said Harriet, round-eyed. For Lord Peregrine Divine was none other than Bertram Hudson.

They sat through the performance as Bertram strode about, ranting and raving and tossing back his hair, which had grown very long.

''What are we going to do?'' asked Harriet as they left after the performance.

''Nothing,'' said the marquess cheerfully. ''We shall return to town and tell his doting mother that her chick is well.''

''But you cannot leave him here!''

''That is exactly what I intend to do. He is no harm to us or society while he is enjoying himself, strutting about the stage and having the time of his life. Poor Jasper St. Clair. I wonder if Bertram took his job. Come along, my sweeting. We have this night all to ourselves. No Aunt Rebecca, no Bertram, and no Cordelia.''

The landlord of the posting house was waiting for them in the courtyard.

''Fine evening, Mr. Hoskins,'' said the marquess

cheerfully. He jumped down and lifted Harriet from the carriage.

"I have a bit o' trouble, my lord. All my private parlors are taken by gentlemen, and I could not put a duchess like her in the common dining room. So when she says she's an old friend o' yourn, I said she could share your parlor for supper, but I don't know as how I've done the right thing."

"Duchess?" said the marquess crossly. "Which duchess?"

"If you wait a bit, I have it wrote down in my book."

"Oh, if our evening is ruined, it's ruined," said the marquess. "Is this mysterious lady ready to dine? I confess to being sharp set myself."

"Above and waiting for you, my lord. I'm that sorry. I wish I hadn't a done it."

"Never mind, Hoskins," said the marquess, relenting. "Come, Harriet. Let us see who we have to keep us company."

The marquess opened the door of the private parlor and stood still on the threshold. Harriet peeped over his arm.

The Dowager Duchess of Macham sat at the table, her bright monkey eyes sparkling with malice.

"Took your time getting here," she grumbled. "Never think of anyone but yourselves, you young people. Don't expect me to pay for this supper. Told 'em to charge it to you. If you hadn't been so tardy in your famous rescue, I might have been able to rescue more of my goods. But selfish. That's what this generation is."

"I cannot stand this," muttered the marquess. "Are we never to be alone again?"

"We have the rest of our lives together," murmured Harriet.

"So we have!" said the marquess, brightening. "So we have!"

So he took his place at the table, smiled lovingly at the old duchess, and said mildly, "I should have let you burn, you horrible woman. Pass the salt."